"Why are we here?" David asked.

"We are here to visit your grave." Isaac replied.

"You mean I'm dead?" David asked.

"Yes, you are dead." Isaac replied.

"I don't remember dying." David said.

"I know that's why we are here." Isaac replied.

"Do you remember your mom and dad?" Isaac asked.

"Yes I do remember my mom and dad!" David exclaimed.

"Do you remember Santa Claus Indiana?" Isaac asked.

"Yes, I do remember Santa Claus Indiana." David replied.

"Did something happen here?" David asked.

"Yes, something really good happened here." Isaac replied.

"Do you remember me David?" Sarah asked.

"Yes, you are Isaac's sister." David replied.

David looked at Isaac and said, "Yes, I'm starting to remember now…."

THE SPECTACLES OF ETERNITY

DAVID L MARSDEN

authorHOUSE®

AuthorHouse™
1663 Liberty Drive
Bloomington, IN 47403
www.authorhouse.com
Phone: 1-800-839-8640

First published by AuthorHouse 8/6/2012

ISBN: 978-1-4634-3426-7 (e)
ISBN: 978-1-4634-3425-0 (sc)

Library of Congress Control Number: 2011911535

Printed in the United States of America

This book is dedicated to the memory of
Frank and Elizabeth Marsden.

TABLE OF CONTENTS

Chapter One
The Ghost in My House

"BE QUIET!" Isaac said.

"Why?" replied David.

"If your Father hears us up here, he will be mad that you have me in your bedroom without permission!" exclaimed Isaac.

The creaking on the stairway let David and Isaac know that David's father was already on his way up to check on his son.

"Now I have gotten you into trouble David!" exclaimed Isaac.

"You do not have to worry about my dad," said David.

"Why?" asked Isaac.

"Because you are dead...a ghost, he can't see you!" replied David.

Then Isaac remembered his death and became angry. He picked up a pillow off the bed and threw it across the room. As David's dad entered the room, he saw the pillow flying through the air.

"Why are you up here throwing things?" inquired David's dad.

Knowing he could not tell his father that a ghost lived in the house with him, he replied,

1

"I was just angry about a bad grade the teacher gave me in Math class."

When Isaac saw the trouble he had gotten David into, he went from angry to sad. Once upon a time he too had a life. Isaac's life ended at a young age, sometime in the late 1800's.

David's dad, who was a tall man with black hair and green eyes, had a deep voice. When John Skinner, which was the father's name, began to speak, it was loud and attention getting. John's glasses would always slide down on his nose when he spoke to loud, forcing him to slide them back up into place on his face. "Listen son, throwing things around is no way to deal with a bad grade, you should study harder and you could get better grades!" Spoke John.

David, who looked much like his father, only smaller, also had black hair and green eyes, David also had a better outlook on life, in that sense, he took after his mother. David and Isaac were the same age, they were both fourteen.

"You are right dad, I will try harder from now on." answered David.

"That's what I like to hear!" said John.

Isaac was now looking out the top bed room window of the house. It was a beautiful day in the town of Santa Claus Indiana. David and his family lived on the out skirts of the town. They lived on a country road, about five miles out of town. It was getting close to summer and the schools were getting ready to release the students for summer vacation.

The skies were blue and the trees were gently blowing with the warm summer wind. The grass was very green, and the creek, which ran by the house David lived in, was peacefully running past the house, as if looking for the next town to flow into.

Isaac remembered a time not so long ago, when he too was alive and going to school.

David's mother, who was in town shopping for groceries, was a very simple woman and liked her life. She enjoyed life in a small town and would not trade it for anything in the world. Her name was Judy, and she loved everything about her little town. Judy, had blonde hair and green eyes, and stood about five foot and four inches. Judy was concerned about David lately, because he seemed to be acting strange. At night she would hear David in his room talking to himself. Sometimes, it was as though he was talking to a person, who was not even in his room. Also, she was hearing footsteps at night, as if someone was walking the halls at night. She would have to talk with him in the near future about his strange behavior.

Back at the Skinner's house, Isaac was tired of sticking around the bedroom and ready to go outside and look for adventure.

"Come on' let's get out of here and do something!" Isaac shouted.

David agreed to go outside in order to avoid any more trouble with his father.

"Lets' go down to the creek and follow it downstream a couple of miles." Isaac said.

"Why do you want to go down by the creek?" David asked.

"A couple of miles down the creek; is the house where I used to live over one hundred years ago!" Exclaimed Isaac, who was getting excited to show David where he used to live. The present date was June of 2011.

David and Isaac headed down stairs and out the door. Mr. Skinner felt the living room get cold.

He could not figure out why. After Isaac left the house, the living room went back to its normal temperature.

The two boys ran down the front porch steps and headed for the creek. After reaching the creek, they followed the creek for about two miles. Within their sight stood an old farm house, which had an old red barn. The house appeared worn down and not lived in for years. Isaac looked at the house and exclaimed, "That is the house where I was born and lived until my death!"

"I bet it was a lot better looking then." David said.

"Yes it was." Isaac said sadly.

"Do you remember how we met?" David asked.

"Yes, we met at the old town graveyard." Isaac answered.

Out beyond the farm house were fields of corn blowing in the warm summer breeze. Isaac seemed to be in deep thought. David headed for the old farm house and when he arrived he went inside to take a look. Inside the house the old floor boards were creaking under the weight of David's shoes. Isaac followed David into the house. In David's mind the house was long ago abandoned. In Isaac's mind, the house was still full of life. Isaac could still see his mom working in the kitchen and his sister playing in the living room. He also could see his dad working in the fields. He had a happy and content life. As David was moving through the house looking at each and every room, Isaac was thinking about his life and how it ended.

While roaming through the house, David found an old pocket watch. It was old and rusty.

"Give me that!" Isaac said.

"Is it yours?" David asked.

"It was my dad's watch." Said Isaac

"Did you like your dad?" Asked David

"Yes, my dad was a good man and he missed me very much when I died." Said Isaac

About one year ago from today, the day that Isaac and David were going through the old farm house and barn, is the day that Isaac and David met each other at the old town graveyard.

David was taking a short cut home from school and decided to cut through the old graveyard. It was a summer day and a warm summer wind was blowing. As David was cutting through the graveyard he decided to climb the fence at the graveyard, rather than walk around to the entrance. While climbing the fence, he got his foot caught on the top part of the fence and fell into the graveyard. The fall did not hurt David, nor was he very concerned about it. What he did not know was that his wallet fell out of his pocket during the fall. Once David got to the exit of the graveyard, he notices that his wallet was missing. Immediately, he headed back into the graveyard to look for his wallet. David spent a long time looking for his wallet and before he knew it, it was getting dark. He was not concerned about the night coming on, because his wallet contained some things which were important to him. Before long, it was totally dark and he could see only what the moonlight allowed him to see. Groping around on the ground, in the graveyard, in the area which he thought that he had lost his wallet, he thought that he heard movement a few yards away. While looking in the direction that the sound came from, he saw a glowing light. While looking at the light, he noticed it was moving. With a closer look, he saw someone in the light. Suddenly, the light started moving towards him. David was getting scared! He got to his feet and started backing up as the light continued to move towards him. No matter how far he backed up, the light continued to follow him. Finally, he stopped backing up and stared at the light and the person in the light, at least he thought it was a human.

"Do not be afraid. I am not going to hurt you." A voice said, in a calm manner.

"Who or what are you and what do you want from me?" David said in a shaky voice.

"I am lost and need a friend." The person in the light replied.

As the person in the light came closer; David noticed that the boy looked about fourteen years old. David was also that age. However, the boy looked pale, and as the boy drew nearer to David, the air around the boy felt very cold.

"Stay where you are. I have seen enough scary movies to know that you are a ghost" Shouted David fearfully.

"You are not like the others I have met, you can really see me." Spoke the ghost, in a surprised manner.

"I can see you alright and you are dead!" David exclaimed.

"I need your help." The ghost said.

"How can I help you?" David asked.

"You need to help me find something." The ghost said.

"What do you need to find?" David asked.

"My spectacles," The ghost replied.

"How can I help?" David asked.

"You can dig my body up and find a letter that is in my pocket." The dead boy replied.

"What is your name?" Asked David

"My name is Isaac and I was alive over one hundred years ago." The ghost replied.

"I can't dig your body up tonight, it's too late!" David exclaimed.

"That is alright, I can go home with you for tonight." The ghost boy replied.

"What will I tell my parent's?" David asked.

"You won't have to tell them anything' they can't see me!" Isaac exclaimed.

"Why can I see you?" David asked.

"I guess it was meant to be." The ghost boy answered.

So, the two boys left the graveyard and headed off to David's house. When they arrived at the house, they quietly walked in the front door and even more quietly walked up the stairs to David's room.

"Now lie down and go to sleep." David said.

"I don't need sleep, I am dead!" Isaac exclaimed.

David's house was quiet. When he had arrived home, he explained to his parent's that he had lost his wallet, and that was why he was late getting home. Later that night, the house was quiet. Isaac was sitting on the roof of the house, thinking back many years in the past when he had died....

CHAPTER TWO
THE DEATH OF ISAAC

L ET US NOW go back to about 1891. This was the year of Isaac's death. However, this was no ordinary death. It was the summer of 1891, and Isaac loved his life. He and his family were very happy and everything was good. Later on in the summer, Isaac started seeing things, which he could not understand.

One day during the late morning hours, when Isaac was taking a walk down by the creek, a storm approached out of what seemed to be nowhere. The wind picked up and the clouds became darker. Isaac looked toward the sky and watched as a tornado came out of the dark clouds. Fearfully, his first thought was to head back home, but the tornado was to close and he had to find shelter immediately. The only thing he could think of doing was going down the bank of the creek and lying flat, hoping that the tornado would not get too close. The tornado touched ground about one mile from where Isaac was. It headed in Isaac's direction, destroying everything in its path. When the tornado was a quarter of a mile from Isaac, it stopped. The tornado hung in the clouds, but did not move any farther.

Isaac was scared to death. He waited for awhile and then wondered what was going on. It had been too long, and the storm should have past by now. Isaac stood up on the bank of the creek, and took a look.

What he saw scared him even more, the tornado was suspended in mid air, and was not moving at all!

As he watched the tornado, a dark hooded figure came out of it, and floated to the ground in front of Isaac. The hooded figure walked until he was looking at Isaac from on top of the creek bank.

The figure had no face, and no hands or feet, it just floated. Isaac was terrified!

"What are you?" Isaac asked.

"I am the monsters that you see in your night mares and the feeling you get when you see something dead." The dark thing said.

"Why do you come to me?" Isaac asked.

"I have come to warn you."The dark thing said.

"Warn me of what?" Isaac inquired.

"Death will be coming for you." The dark thing replied.

"Why do you tell me this?" Isaac asked fearfully.

"Listen boy, when you die, you will become a being that lives between life and death, and you will be visited by an entity." The dark spirit replied.

"What do you mean?" Isaac continued.

"A being known by your kind as an angel." Answered the dark thing.

"Why?" Isaac asked.

"The angel will ask you to do something for it." The dark thing said.

"Do not listen to the angel if you value your soul." The dark thing continued.

"Why?"Isaac asked.

"My time is up and I must go." The dark thing said.

"Please tell me what the angel will want!" Isaac exclaimed.

"If you help the angel, I will cast your soul into everlasting darkness!" The dark spirit said.

The dark spirit floated back into the storm, the tornado went back up into the clouds and the storm ended. Isaac was so scared that he began to cry as he ran back towards the farm where he lived. Isaac knew winter was only a few months away and could not even imagine being dead by then!

Isaac's father was at home, as was his mother, worried to death about their son. Isaac's father was a short man, with blonde hair and blue eyes. He was very stocky and was no stranger to hard work on a farm in the 1800's. He began shouting Isaac's name, as he was walking down a dirt road looking for his son. His shouting was very loud and his mouth was hidden by his bushy beard and mustache.

Isaac's mother was also worried, but she had to stay home with her ten year old daughter Sarah.

The Smiths were Amish and had a deep faith in God. Rebecca told her daughter not to worry, that God would keep Isaac safe. Isaac's father continued shouting and hoping the tornado did not kill his son.

"Isaac...Isaac!" John Smith shouted.

John saw the storm, and it seemed to him that he had never seen a storm end that way. This was the first time he ever saw anything like it, and could not explain it away in his mind.

After walking a while, and yelling a lot, John saw Isaac running down the dirt road towards him.

Isaac saw his father and began shouting, "Father!"

"Where on earth have you been boy?" His father said.

"Down by the creek hiding from the storm!" Isaac exclaimed.

"You could have been killed!" His father said.

"Yes, but I wasn't." Isaac replied.

John and Isaac turned around and headed back towards their farmhouse. When they arrived Rebecca did not know whether to be happy or mad at Isaac. Sarah was just happy to see her big brother.

Later that night safe in his bed, Isaac thought about what he had seen and heard and decided that it was just his imagination mixed with fear playing tricks on his mind.

As Isaac was getting sleepy, the only other thing on his mind was that tomorrow his whole family was going into town in the horse and buggy, for church, and a picnic. The trip into town made him happy. While in town Isaac could see some of his friends.

Well, first days past and then months. Now it was late October, and everybody could tell that winter was on the way. The corn husk had turned brown, and the nights were coming earlier. It was also becoming colder by the day.

One morning in October, Isaac was outside with his sister Sarah. They were Climbing trees. Isaac and Sarah loved to climb trees, because besides farm work, there was not a lot to do. Later that night, Isaac took sick and began running a fever.

While Isaac was suffering through his fever and angel came to him. The angel came in the form of a bright light. When the light reached Isaac's bed it took form. The angel appeared in the form of a woman. The angel had dark flowing hair and a robe made of light. The look on her face was one of kindness and compassion. Her eye's reflected a world beyond the one that humans know.

"I am a messenger from the Land of the Good." The angel said.

Isaac opened his eyes and saw how beautiful the angel was. Isaac knew that he was going to die. He remembered what the dark being had told him some months before. Isaac was afraid to die and he told the angel how he felt.

"Do not be afraid." Said the angel, whose name was Elizabeth.

"You have been chosen to fulfill a very important job." The angel continued.

"What job?" Isaac asked in a weak voice.

"To protect The Spectacles of Eternity," The angel answered.

"Why?" Isaac asked.

"You were chosen." The angel replied.

"Why was I chosen?" Isaac asked.

"It is the will of the King." The angel answered.

"What are The Spectacles of Eternity?" Isaac asked.

"You will know when you leave your body." Replied the angel

"You will come with me to the Land of the Good." The angel continued.

"I am afraid to die!" Isaac cried in a weak voice.

"I will be with you to help you through it." The angel said.

The compassion and love on the angel's face comforted Isaac and made him feel safe and warm.

Knowing that Isaac was going to die, Isaac's parents were in the room with him. They could not see the angel, who was with Isaac. It was about ten o'clock in the evening and earlier that day, Isaac's parents had called on the town doctor. When the doctor told John that Isaac had pneumonia, and it was in his lungs, John knew Isaac was not going to live. After the doctor informed the family of the bad news, John called on the minister, who was at present also in Isaac's room.

"Why am I the only one that can see you?" Isaac asked the angel.

"Because part of you is in this world and the other is in my world." The angel answered.

Suddenly, Isaac's spirit left his body. The angel took his hand and stayed with him as he watched his Parent's. Rebecca was crying and John was trying to comfort her. Sarah was not in the room. Isaac went with the angel into the next room where Sarah was sitting on wooden chair. Isaac wanted to hug his sister good bye, but his arms went right through her. Sarah felt a cold blast of air, but could not see her brother. The angel told Isaac that he could see them, but they could not see him.

"You must let go of this world and come with me." The angel said.

"I do not want to leave my family." Isaac said sadly.

"You will be with them again in due time." The angel replied.

"Where do I have to go?" Isaac asked.

"Take my hand and I will show you." The angel replied.

Isaac took the angels hand, and they both floated up through the ceiling of the house and continued up into the clouds. It was a cold night, but Isaac could not feel the cold, only the warmth that radiated from the angel. The sky was clear and full of stars. The angel took Isaac up among the stars. Isaac watched in wonder of how beautiful the stars were.

"So Heaven is up in the sky?" Isaac asked.

"Heaven is everywhere." Replied the angel

"Then why are we in the sky?" Isaac asked.

"I just wanted you to see the wonder of the stars." The angel replied.

"Heaven is in you and all around you." The angel continued.

The angel continued to take Isaac to different levels of

existence. Isaac saw many different lands and many different types of beings. Some of the beings looked like humans and others did not look like humans at all. One of the lands the angel took him to was Nowhere Land. The angel told Isaac this land has lived in peace every since the downfall of "King Addictions."

In some of the other lands, animals ruled and there were no humans. In another land, nothing was what a human would call normal. This land was created by other children who had died, and now live in the land of their dreams. In the land of the children, there was no pain or sadness, only joy and security.

After the angel finished showing Isaac all of the sights, it was time to visit the "Land of the Good." Isaac knew that the next land was where he would meet the one who created him.

Chapter Three
A Visit to the "Land of the Good"

THE ANGEL ELIZABETH brought Isaac into the "Land of the Good." The land had huge snow covered mountains, blue skies, and clear blue lakes. The air was not touched by pollution and was very fresh. The Sun was bright and warm in the "Land of the Good." Isaac could see thousands of angels flying into and away from this land.

"Before you meet the good spirit, I want you to see some people." The angel said.

The angel flew Isaac to a green pasture below the mountains and down to a huge tree, which was full of bright green leaves. When Isaac and the angel landed, Isaac heard a familiar voice call for him. "Hello Isaac, it is good to see you again." Spoke a young man, with curly blonde hair.

Isaac took a look at the person talking to him, and realized it was his grandfather, only younger! Isaac became very excited, every since his grandfather had died, he had missed him very much. Isaac noticed a woman standing next to his grandfather, and realized it was his grandmother, only younger!"

"I missed you so much!" Isaac said to his grandparents.

"We missed you to Isaac." The grandfather said.

Isaac's grandfather informed Isaac that when a person leaves the old world and comes to this place, they are young again. Isaac's grand fathers name was Hank and His grandmother's name was Gertrude. They had a happy and long life together and were now together with each other in the afterlife.

The angel told Isaac it was time to go. Isaac said good bye to his grandparents and went with the angel. Elizabeth flew Isaac to the top of the biggest mountain in the land. On top of the mountain was a crystal clear castle. As the angel flew towards the castle, the castle doors opened to let her and Isaac into the castle. Once in the castle, the angel landed with Isaac.

"You must go alone from here to see the Boss." Elizabeth said.

"Why?" Isaac asked.

"The Boss only wants to talk to you." The angel replied.

Isaac began walking towards the big white door, which the angel pointed him to. When he reached the door he opened it and walked in. As soon as he walked in he fell down into darkness.

He was falling fast and it seemed to have no end. Finally, he stopped in what felt like mid air, but was a dark cloud. On the cloud he saw another spirit. The spirit was very sad and depressed looking. Isaac also heard other people crying as if they were in great pain. The spirit, who took the form of a large man with dark black hair and deep set brown eyes asked,

"Why are you here boy?"

"I don't know." Isaac answered.

"You are in the "Void of Sadness," The angel said.

"I was going to talk to the Boss!" Isaac said.

"Before anyone can see the Boss, they must enter the Void of Sadness." Spoke the angel.

"What is the Void of Sadness?" Isaac asked.

"It is the void where all human sadness and pain ends up." Answered the angel

"Who are you?" Isaac asked.

"I am the keeper of the Void of Sadness." The angel said.

"There is too much sadness in the human race, so we take it!" The angel continued.

"Why?" Isaac asked.

"Because we hear it, and send angels to help humans." The angel replied.

"So there are more than you that do this job?" Isaac asked.

"Many!" The angel exclaimed.

"How do you help people?" Isaac inquired.

"We send spirits like you, back in the dreams of your loved ones." The angel said.

"That way you can let your loved ones know you are happy and safe." The angel continued.

"You mean I can go back and see my sister Sarah?" Isaac asked.

"You can go back to each one of your family members." The angel replied.

"Would you like to go back now, before you go see the Boss?" The angel asked.

"Oh Yes!" Isaac exclaimed.

"Very well, close your eyes." The sad looking angel said.

Back at Isaac's parent's house, several days after his burial, Sarah was fast asleep in her bed. She began dreaming of Isaac and the things they use to do together. In her dream she was down by the creek fishing with Isaac. Suddenly,

Isaac turned to his sister and said, "I love you and miss you Sarah."

Sarah stirred in her sleep. In her dream she looked at her brother and began to cry.

"Is it really you Isaac?" She asked.

"Yes, it is really me Sis." Isaac replied.

"How can this be?" Sarah exclaimed.

"They let me come back to tell you I am OK." Isaac answered.

"Will I ever see you again?" Sarah asked.

"One day our whole family will be together again, in the "Land of the Good." Isaac replied.

"That makes me happy!" Sarah exclaimed.

"In the mean time, grow up and never give up on your dreams." Isaac said.

"Will you be back in my dreams Isaac?" Sarah asked.

"I will try." Isaac replied.

"Good bye Isaac, I love you." Sarah said.

"Good bye and I will see you again!" Isaac exclaimed.

Isaac had already visited his parents and was back in the "Void of Sadness." He was now ready to meet the one called the Boss. Isaac said good bye to the sad looking angel in the "Void of Sadness," and floated up out of the void and in through the door to learn of his destiny.

Isaac entered the chamber of the Boss. When he entered he did not see any body. Isaac looked around and saw a white room. In the room were chairs and a desk.

"Come in Isaac!" Spoke a loud thunderous voice.

"Where are you sir?" Isaac asked.

"I am everywhere and in everything!" The voice answered.

"Did you want to see me for a reason?" Isaac asked.

"I have something for you to guard for me." The voice replied.

"Does it have anything to do with a pair of spectacles?" Isaac asked.

"Yes, the Spectacles of Eternity." The voice replied.

"For centuries of your earth's time, I have been moving the spectacles in and out of different worlds." The thunderous voice continued.

"Why have you been hiding them?" Isaac asked.

"We must keep my son from getting them." The voice replied.

"Who is your Son?" Isaac asked.

"He is known by many names." The thunderous voice answered.

"What do you call him?" asked Isaac.

"I call him the Dark One." The voice replied.

"Some know him as the Devil or Lucifer." The voice continued.

"Yes' I was taught about him at church." Isaac said.

"I have chosen you because you are destined to work for me." The voice said.

"Some call me God; some call me the Great White Spirit." The voice continued.

"What do you want me to call you?" Isaac asked.

"You can just call me the Boss." The voice replied.

"I am also the truth, and not everybody likes the truth." The Boss continued.

"Why don't you want your Son to have the spectacles?" Isaac asked.

"Because when people wear them, they see the truth about life." The Boss answered.

"What do they see?" Isaac asked.

"You will find out soon enough." The Boss said.

"Where are they now?" Isaac asked.

"You do not need to know that until the year 2010." The Boss answered.

"What shall I do in the meantime?" Isaac asked.

"You will stay in the "Land of the Good" for now." The Boss replied.

"A letter will be hidden in your grave sometime in 2010." The Boss continued.

"Why at my grave?" Isaac asked.

"Before that time, my dark Son will have already searched your grave, without finding them." The Boss replied.

"He will be looking elsewhere by then." The Boss continued.

"What will be in the letter?" Isaac asked.

"You will see when you read it." The Boss answered.

So, Isaac stayed in the "Land of the Good" for many years, but human years and the Bosses idea of time were much different! While in the "Land of the Good," Isaac stayed with his grandparents and a pet dog, which he had while still alive. The dog died when Isaac was only eight years old. The dogs name was Whiskers. Also, there was a cat, which died when Isaac was five. The cats name was Rocky. So for the time Isaac spent in the "Land of the Good," he spent living in a House of clear crystal, and running in green fields, under sunny skies, with Whiskers and Rocky. Isaac spent much time with his grandparents. His grand pa told him old and glorious stories of the adventures that he had while growing up on the old farm in Indiana. Isaac had never been happier. In the "Land of the Good," there was no death, no suffering and no pain. There was no worry about war or disease. Everything in the "Land of the Good" was like a wonderful dream, which never ended!

After spending some time in the "Land of the Good," Isaac was rejoined with his mother and father. His mother and father lived to a ripe old age and then died a natural death. However, even though he knew his sister had died, he did not see Sarah with his mother and father in the "Land of the Good." Isaac wondered where his sister could be if not with his family.

While in the "Land of the Good," he learned that pets were angels in animal suits, and death really wasn't the end. The time came for Isaac to go back to his grave and wait for orders. It was during this time that he met David.

Chapter Four

David is taken by Hate

It was starting to get dark and David told Isaac that it was time to go back to the Skinner's home for the night.

"Let's go then." Isaac said.

"You look sad." David replied.

"I was just thinking about the days when my family and I lived here." Isaac said.

Both of the boys headed back to the house. When they got there, David walked in the front door and saw his mother and father sitting in the living room watching television.

"Where were you tonight young man?" His mother asked.

"Yeah, it's nine o 'clock at night!" His father exclaimed.

Isaac was standing right next to David, but of course, David's mom and dad could not see Isaac, because Isaac was a ghost.

"I was just out exploring." David answered.

"Well, come in and make sure you close the door." David's mom said.

"Yeah, it feels like you let a cold draft in the house." Mr. Skinner said.

David told his parents that he had checked the door and

it was closed tight, then he said good night and proceeded to go upstairs with Isaac. Once David was in his room he closed the door.

"Every time we come into the house they feel cold!" Exclaimed David

"It's not my fault, it comes with being dead!" Isaac said, with an angry look on his face.

"I am sorry." David said.

"It's OK. I'm used to it." Isaac answered.

"Tomorrow night we have to dig up my grave and get into my casket." Isaac continued.

"That sounds scary!" David replied.

"Then you need to open my casket and find the letter in my pocket." Isaac said.

"What is the letter about?" asked David.

"It is a letter that the Boss wrote for me." Isaac replied.

"Why didn't you just get the spectacles from the Boss?" David asked.

"It was too dangerous to keep them on me." Isaac answered.

"Why?" Inquired David

"There are dark forces trying to stop any human from wearing the spectacles." Isaac replied.

"You mean like demons!" David exclaimed.

"Yes' like demons." Isaac replied.

"Well' that leaves me out." David said.

"Why?" Isaac asked.

"There is no way I want to get demons mad at me!" David exclaimed, in a scared voice.

"Sorry' you have no choice." Isaac replied.

"What do you mean?" asked David.

"You have been chosen." Isaac replied.

"Chosen by who?" asked David, who was now getting angry.

"You have been chosen by the Boss." Isaac answered.

"Who is the Boss?" David asked.

"He is the one who created you." Isaac responded.

"Are you telling me I have been chosen by God?" asked David.

"Yes." Isaac replied.

"I can't even get chosen for a spelling bee at school." David said.

"This is different!" Isaac exclaimed.

"Why does he want me?" asked David.

"He wants you to wear the spectacles." The ghost replied.

"Why?" asked David.

"So you can see the truth and tell other humans about it." Isaac answered.

"The truth is that I'm scared to death!" exclaimed David.

"Come on, I will tell you more on the way to the grave yard." Isaac said.

The two boys waited until David's mom and dad were in bed, and then they quietly headed for the hallway and then the stairs. In minutes, they were down the stairs and out the back door. Once outside, they headed for the grave yard. It was dark, but the moon offered them some light. They followed the creek to the grave yard. Once in the grave yard they headed for Isaac's grave.

On the way to the grave, they heard somebody crying.

"Do you hear that Isaac?" asked David.

"Yes' I do hear it!" exclaimed Isaac.

"Let's check it out." David said.

"Wait!" Isaac exclaimed.

"Why?" David asked.

"Listen' can you hear where it is coming from?" Isaac asked.

"Over there by that tree!" Isaac exclaimed.

The two boys saw what looked like a small child dressed in a dark robe. David approached the child and asked "Why are you crying?"

At that point the child turned and looked at David and had a large evil grin on its face.

"I have a present for you human!" The dark spirit said.

Isaac saw the child's face and knew that it was from the dark world.

"David, get away from the child!" Isaac shouted.

When David turned around to ask Isaac why, the child touch him on one of his legs, and David vanished. David was sent to the dark world. Isaac ran up to the dark child, and looked the child in the eyes and asked, "What did you do with my friend?"

"Your friend is in the dark land and now belongs to my master!" The dark thing exclaimed.

"Who are you evil one?" Isaac inquired.

"I am called many names, but in the dark world, I am known as "Hate."

"You will return my friend or I will call on the Boss to take revenge." Isaac said.

"The Boss cannot touch me; he must let life take its course." "Hate" shouted.

With in the next minute "Hate" was gone! And Isaac was alone in the graveyard. Isaac was alone and scared, and did not know what to do next. While trying to think of something, a bright light appeared to him.

"Isaac' do not be afraid, I will help you find David and get the spectacles." The light said.

Isaac was looking at the light, and in the light he saw his sister Sarah! The light around Sarah dimmed, and she walked out of the light and ran up to Isaac and hugged him.

After the hug, Isaac looked at his sister and asked her what she was doing here in a grave yard in Santa Claus Indiana.

"I have been with the Boss since my death." Sarah said.

"So that is why I never saw you in the "Land of the Good" with mom and dad." Isaac replied.

"Yes, the Boss knew all along that you would need my help." Sarah said.

"We need to get that letter out of my casket and go help David!" Isaac exclaimed.

"There is no need; I already took the letter from your casket." Sarah said.

Under the stars on a cool summer's night, Isaac and Sarah held hands and thought of the day when they were still alive on this earth, and how short their time had been in this life. They were both sad there life on earth was over. They both knew how short a walk their life was, and hoped that people who were still in this life are making every day count.

"Where do we start to look for David?" Sarah asked.

"David is in Hell." Isaac replied.

"How can we get to him?" Sarah asked.

"We must go to the Land of the Opposites." Isaac answered.

"Let's go then!" exclaimed Sarah.

"Take my hand and fly with me to a different land, not of this earth." Spoke Isaac.

When Sarah took Isaac's hand, a warm light surrounded both of them. The light began to move through many different lands, which were not of this earth. The light moved too fast for the human eye to see, and in an instant they were in the "Land of the Opposites." When Sarah and Isaac arrived they were met by a guard, who guarded the gate of entrance into the "Land of the Opposites." The guard looked quite odd. One half of the guard was a man and the other half was a woman!

"Halt, who goes there," exclaimed the male guard.

"I am Isaac, sent by the Boss." Replied Isaac

"This is my sister Sarah." Isaac continued.

"The Boss sent you?" The male side of the guard asked.

"Yes." Isaac replied.

"Why are you half man and half woman?" Sarah asked.

"Two halves make a whole." The female side of the guard replied.

"That makes sense." Sarah replied.

"Since you were sent by the Boss, you may enter." The male side of the guard replied.

Every being in every land of life, knew who the Boss was. So, the guard opened the gate and let Isaac, and his sister, enter. When they entered the "Land of the Opposites," Isaac and Sarah were surprised. As they looked upon the land, it was night and day at the same time! They saw the sun and the stars at the same time! In the part of the land that was day, they saw a village, which had buildings made of oak wood. The buildings were well kept and looked as if they were straight out of a fairy tale. The night part of the land was dark, with a full moon. Some people in this part of the land were out looking at stars and talking, and others were sleeping.

"Let's go ask somebody where the portal to Hell is!" Sarah exclaimed.

So, Isaac and Sarah walked up to the first building they saw and went in. The building they went into appeared to be a general store. The store had canned goods and flour. The store also had a department with camping supplies and equipment. It was indeed a general store with many different items for sale. Isaac saw a store clerk, as he was walking around the store. The clerk had on jeans and a T-shirt, and an apron. He was at least six feet tall and had a dark bushy beard and mustache. The clerk seemed to be busy arranging some canned goods on a shelf.

"Excuse me." Isaac said.

The big man turned around and saw Isaac. His eyes were very sincere, as was his voice.

"Hello, how may I help you?" The man said

"My name is Isaac, and this is my sister Sarah." Isaac replied.

"My name is half." The man said.

"Why is that your name?" Sarah inquired.

"Because my other half is busy in the kitchen." The man answered.

"How may I help you?" asked the man.

"We seek the portal to Hell." Isaac answered.

"Why would you want to know that?" The man asked.

"We are going to find a friend we lost." Sarah answered.

"Many people have gone through Hell seeking answers, and have never returned!" The man exclaimed.

"We know who we are looking for." Isaac said.

"Hell is the land where all of the opposites are in a constant state of confusion." The man said.

"We know." Isaac returned.

"The portal to Hell can be found on top of the mountain of the opposites." The man said.

"It's on the top of the mountain?" Sarah asked.

"Yes, right in the middle on the top of the mountain." The man replied.

"Once you enter the portal there is only confusion." The man continued.

"How do you know all of this?" Isaac asked.

"I had to go to Hell to find a friend." The man said.

"Did you get your friend out of Hell?" Isaac inquired.

"No, he refused to let go of his hate." The man replied.

"We could use some of your camping gear." Isaac said.

Half agreed and went to the camping department of the store. While he was in the camping department showing Isaac some tents, the phone rang. Half answered the phone, while Isaac and Sarah kept looking for things they would need for the trip up the mountain. The "Land of the Opposites" was not like the human world. Spirit's powers did not work in this land. They would have to physically climb the mountain.

After talking on the phone for a few minutes, half walked over to talk with Isaac and Sarah.

"That was the Boss on the phone." The man said.

"What did he want?" Isaac asked.

"He said you are not to go into Hell." The man answered.

"Why?" Sarah asked.

"He said he wants you to go back to the human grave yard and wait." The man said.

So, Isaac and Sarah returned to the grave yard and waited. The world of humans was different than the "Land of the Opposites." In the "Land of the Opposites", everyone and everything had another half to it. When the two halves were brought together, they formed a happy medium and all was at peace. The "Land of the Opposites" had moderation. The world of humans had peace also, but they also had confusion.

Hell had no moderation or peace, only confusion and the feeling of being lost. The beings, which existed in Hell, thrived on chaos and confusion to torture the souls that were lost there. Speaking of Hell, at this time, David was still in Hell. The Bosses dark son needed to hold David there, to keep him from helping Isaac find "The Spectacles of Eternity"!

CHAPTER FIVE
WHISKERS MEETS DAVID IN HELL

WHEN DAVID WOKE up, he found himself in what appeared to be a large cave, with torches all along the wall. The cave was a holding area of Hell. David Shouted,

"Where am I?"

"You are in Hell!" A loud deep voice replied.

"Who are you?" David asked.

A deep voice replied, and it echoed throughout the cave.

"I am the Dark One, ruler of all realms of existence!"

"What do you want from me?" David asked.

"You have interfered with my plans and now you must pay." The voice replied.

"I was just trying to help a friend!" David exclaimed.

"When I am done with some urgent work, I will be back for you." The voice continued.

"I am not dead!" Shouted David

"Not yet, but you soon will be." The Dark One replied.

"Why do you want to kill me?" David asked.

"You human beings are pathetic." The Dark One replied.

"But, why kill me?" David asked.

"You have stuck your pathetic nose into a spiritual struggle." The voice answered.

"I will soon kill you, and cast your soul into the pit of Hell." The voice continued.

"Can't you just let me go?" David asked.

"Silence!" the Dark One shouted.

The Dark One announced his leaving, but said he would be back. As the Dark One was leaving his voice could be heard, saying, "Death, destruction, darkness for all...."

David found a spot and sat down in the dirt of the cave. Suddenly, he saw a black dog walking towards him.

"What is a dog doing in Hell?" He thought to himself.

The dog walked up to him and spoke, "Hello, my name is Whiskers."

"You talk?" David asked.

"Sure I do, haven't you ever seen an angel in a dog suit?" The dog asked.

"Why are you here?" David asked.

"To help you escape from Hell!" Whiskers exclaimed.

"How will you do that?" David asked.

"Just grab a hold of my tail and hold on." Whiskers replied.

"Are you just going to fly me out?" David asked.

"Yes, we just fly out of here." The dog replied.

"Then what are we waiting for?" David asked.

"We must first fly through a small part of Hell." Whiskers answered.

"I would rather not." David said.

"There is no other way." The dog replied.

So, David grabbed the dog's tail, and said, "Let's get this over with!"

Upon grabbing whisker's tail, a bright light surrounded David and the dog, and in no time they were both in the cave flying!

"You will hear sounds of great suffering coming from the souls in Hell." Whiskers said.

"You mean from the fire?" David asked.

"Hell is not fire, it is emotional turmoil." The dog replied.

"What do you mean?" David asked.

"It is people who were trapped in bad situations in life." The dog answered.

"I thought that was over when you died." David said.

"Some sad things are hard to escape." The dog replied.

"What do you mean?" David asked.

"Some people either can't or won't let go of sad things that happen in life." The dog said.

"So they are punished for it?" David asked.

"Hell is just a continuation of it." Whiskers replied.

While flying through Hell, David looked down into a pit in Hell, and saw a man, who was swinging his arms and fist at what appeared to be large animals trying to bite his skin off. Upon closer look, David saw the things were flying, they had wings. One of the things began sniffing, like it senses something that it did not like. The flying thing looked up toward Whiskers and David, and grinned.

"What is that thing?" David asked.

"It is a demon." Whiskers said.

"It looks like it sees us." David asked.

"It smells us." Whiskers replied.

The demon began flying towards David and Whiskers. When it came closer it could be seen for what it was. The thing had a human head, with horns. It's eye's were as red as fire and its teeth were long and sharp. The demon hung in mid-air for awhile sniffing, and then left.

"Why are those demons ripping that mans skin off?" David asked.

"Demons torment souls." Whiskers replied.

"That is not a man?" David asked.

"It is the man's soul." Whiskers replied.

"The skin is growing back after they rip it off!" David exclaimed.

"Like I said, they torment the soul." Whiskers replied.

"They are being misled by the Boss." Whiskers continued.

"What do you mean?" David asked.

"The demons will torture the soul until it lets go of its past life on earth." Whiskers said.

"You mean the soul does not stay in Hell?" David asked.

"After the soul lets go, it will go to the "Land of the Good." Whiskers answered.

"I thought that Hell was for eternity." David said.

"It is not." Whiskers replied.

"The demons are working for the Boss and don't know it." Whiskers continued.

"What do you mean?" David asked.

"They torture the soul so much; they end up setting it free!" Whiskers exclaimed.

"They are angels in a way, they just don't realize it." Whiskers continued.

After the incident with the demon, Whiskers continued flying until he reached the portal to the "Land of the Opposites." Once he reached the portal, Whiskers flew straight up and out into the "Land of the Opposites". David saw that the land was half night and half day. He asked Whiskers why this was so.

"This land is a peaceful land because all the opposites join together." The dog said.

"What do you mean?" David asked.

"Everything in life has another side to it." Whiskers replied.

Whiskers went on to explain to David that the day had the night, and happiness had sadness.

The dog further explained that war had peace, and people have two eyes, two ears, two arms and two legs. Whiskers told David that when these opposites work together, they bring about a balance, a sort of harmony. The dog also told David, that if you eat too much you get sick, and if you eat too little you get sick, but if you eat just the right amount, it is good for you. Whiskers told David that the secret of life is moderation.

After flying through the other worlds, David and Whiskers finally arrived at the grave yard and met up with Isaac and Sarah. The amount of time that David was gone was only about an hour in earth time!

"I am glad you are back, David!" Isaac exclaimed.

"I am too." David replied.

"Did you get the spectacles?" Whiskers asked.

"I don't have them on me." Isaac replied.

"What do you mean you don't have them on you?" Whiskers asked.

"The letter said that an orange cat is wearing the spectacles." Isaac replied.

"Where is this orange cat now?" David asked.

"The cat is in the Rocky Mountains." Isaac replied.

"Why is the cat in the Rocky Mountains?" David asked.

"He is hiding from the Dark One's soldiers." Isaac said.

"You mean we have to climb the Rockies to get the spectacles!" David exclaimed.

"I guess we do." Isaac answered.

"I have to go home and check in with my parents." David said.

"Can I go with you David?" Sarah asked.

"You might as well." David said.

"Good, we can all go!" Isaac exclaimed.

"We need to get going before my parents start to wonder where I am." David said.

So, there they went David, and three ghosts. They all walked through the grave yard and out through the front gate, and headed down the road towards David's house. On the way David was trying to figure how he was going to be able to go to the Rockies. He did not know what he would tell his parents. David had already seen so many things today that were unbelievable.

"Do I have to go with you?" David asked Isaac.

"Yes, we need you to put on the spectacles." Isaac answered.

"Why?" David asked.

"The Boss needs one good human to live one day with the spectacles on." Isaac said.

"The spectacles will show you life through new eyes." Sarah said.

"What do you mean?" David asked.

"You cannot see everything with your human eyes." Isaac answered.

"There are many different plains of existence other than your own." Sarah said.

"The spectacles will show you the truth about life." Isaac said.

"Does the cat we are looking for have a name?" David asked.

"His name is Rocky." Sarah said.

"We can fly you to the Rockies in no time." Isaac said.

CHAPTER SIX
THE THREE GHOST IN MY HOUSE

ONCE DAVID AND his three friends arrived at David's house, they went into the house through the back door. David proceeded to walk into the living room. What David did not know was that Whiskers and Sarah followed right behind him. Mr. and Mr.'s Skinner were on the couch watching television. Whiskers walked in front of the television, stopped for a couple minutes, then walked back into the kitchen.

"What's that horrid smell?" Mr.'s Skinner exclaimed.

"It smells like dog poop." Mr. Skinner replied.

"How can it be dog poop if we don't have a dog?" Mr.'s Skinner replied.

"I don't know, but this whole room smells like poop!" Mr. Skinner exclaimed.

Once back in the kitchen, Whiskers walked up to Isaac, and sat down. Hearing the Skinners talking, Isaac looked at Whiskers and asked.

"You didn't?" Isaac asked.

"Yes' I pooped in the living room." Whiskers answered.

At about the same time, Sarah saw the television and was thrilled!

"What is this?" She exclaimed.

David could not answer Sarah, because she was invisible, and he would look stupid talking to nobody!

Sarah was so excited; the energy coming from her spirit began changing the television channels at random.

Appearing scared, Mr.'s Skinner said, "The television is changing stations by itself!"

"What is causing it?" Mr. Skinner asked.

"I don't know, but it scares me." Mrs. Skinner replied.

David saw what was happening and stood in front of the television set, and motioned Sarah to go into the kitchen with Isaac. Sarah left and the television went back to normal.

"It was just electrical interference." David said nervously

A little shaken up Mr. Skinner replied, "I guess your right David."

While David was talking with his parents, Isaac decided to see what the Skinners had to eat in their kitchen. Sarah was now in the kitchen with Isaac, and decided to help him find some food. Even though Isaac and Sarah were spirits, they still had the human habit of getting hungry. Isaac was looking in the refrigerator, while Sarah was climbing up on a chair to look in some cabinets. Sarah could barely reach the cabinet door, and when she reached it, the door came open and pots and pans began falling out on the floor!

Meanwhile, in the living room, Mr.'s Skinner was so surprised by the noise in the kitchen; she jumped up out of her chair and screamed.

"This house must be haunted!" Mr.'s Skinner exclaimed.

"That is ridiculous." Mr. Skinner replied.

While David's mom and dad were talking, David ran

into the kitchen and saw Sarah up on a chair, looking in the cabinets.

"What in the world are you doing Sarah?" David asked in an angry voice.

"I am just looking for some food." Sarah replied.

"You are making too much noise!" Exclaimed David

"I am sorry!" Sarah said, with sad looking eyes.

"We sometimes forget that we are ghost." Isaac said.

"When do we head for the mountains?" David asked.

"As soon as we get to your bedroom." Isaac answered.

"How long will I be gone?" David asked.

"You will be gone for an hour." Isaac replied.

"You had better take a winter coat David." Sarah said.

"I have one in my closet upstairs." David replied.

David and the three ghosts went up the stairs, and into David's bedroom.

Meanwhile, in the living room downstairs, Mr. Skinner was still trying to calm his wife down after the recent chain of weird events in their house. While his parent's were still discussing the events in the house, David put on his winter coat and Isaac instructed everyone to stand in a circle and take hands. Isaac, David, and the others stood in a circle and held hands. A warm white light formed around all of them, and they suddenly vanished. In the blink of an eye, they were in the Rocky Mountains.

"It's cold up here." David said.

"Do you see that peak at the top of this mountain?" Isaac asked.

"I see it!" David answered.

"There is a cave up there, and Rocky is hiding in it." Isaac continued.

"That's a long way up to the cave." David said anxiously.

"I will fly you up with me." Isaac replied.

The night was cold, and the wind was whipping to and fro. David was already freezing, even with his jacket on. The night was dark, but the moon provided light. Isaac was getting ready to fly David to the peak of the mountain, to go into the cave and find Rocky, suddenly, the moon turned blood red, and a face appeared in it. A voice came from above, it was loud and angry.

"You fool, cease your journey or be destroyed!" shouted the Dark One.

"Who is that?" David asked fearfully.

"It is Hades, Satan, Lucifer; we just call it the Dark One." Isaac replied.

"I command all of the dark forces." The Dark One shouted.

Out of the night sky, came the sound of wings. The sounds were loud and were heading straight for David, and his friends.

"My soldiers are coming to chew you to pieces!" The Dark One shouted.

It was dark and hard to see, David was scared. Isaac appeared calm. The flying soldiers of Hell were getting closer!

"We need to leave now!" David shouted.

"It is too late." Sarah replied.

Another voice came from the wind, but it was the voice of the Boss,

"Isaac' pick up some snow and throw it towards the sky."

Isaac picked up a hand full of snow and threw it up towards the night sky. A great white light came from the snow and lit up the night sky. David and the others could see hundreds of demons flying towards them. The snow, which Isaac threw in the air, then turned into a huge whirl wind.

The demons became caught up in the huge whirl wind, and were swept away into the night.

"This is the work of my Father!" The Dark One shouted.

The face on the moon began to vanish, and a voice spoke with a vanishing tone.

"You will not be this lucky the next time." Spoke the Dark One.

After the ordeal with the dark one, Isaac flew David to the mountain peak. Once on the top of the mountain, David and Isaac walked for a few minutes, and then saw the cave.

"That's the cave!" Isaac exclaimed.

"Let's go in quick so I don't freeze to death." David replied.

While in the cave, Isaac's radiant spirit lit up the cave enough to see inside. David and Isaac walked awhile in the cave, until they heard a sound. They heard a snoring sound.

"Rocky...is that you?" Isaac asked.

Suddenly, the snoring stopped and a voice came from a little further in the cave.

"Whose there?" The voice shouted.

"It's me Rocky." Isaac shouted.

"I am sorry I don't know any me's?" Rocky replied.

"It's me, Isaac." Isaac replied.

"Thank God. I thought it was another demon." Rocky said.

"The demons are gone for now." Isaac replied.

When David and Isaac reached the back of the cave, they saw an orange cat, with spectacles on!

"I can see you are a good person David!" The cat exclaimed.

"How can you tell that?" David asked.

"I am wearing the spectacles. I see the truth." The cat answered.

"How long have you been up here?" Isaac asked.

"I've been going from cave to cave, hiding from regular demons for a week." Rocky replied.

"Do you mean more than one demon?" Isaac asked.

"Yes." Rocky replied.

"What do you mean regular demons?" David inquired.

"Hades has his more powerful soldiers." Isaac said.

"The regular demons are the less powerful ones." Isaac continued.

"Who are they?" David asked.

"Among the many powerful ones are "Hate" and "Deceit." Isaac answered.

"Why are they more powerful?" David asked.

"They can control a person's feelings." Isaac answered.

"We have no more time to talk!" Rocky said.

"He's right' we need to leave now." Isaac said.

Isaac picked up Rocky, and grabbed David's hand. Isaac flew them both out of the cave and down to where Whiskers and Sarah were waiting.

"What an adorable kitty!" Sarah exclaimed.

"I'm a cat, not a kitty." Rocky said, in an angry way.

"I need to get back home before my parent's find out I'm gone." David said.

"David is right!" Isaac exclaimed.

David and the four ghosts stood in a circle, held hands and waited. In a few seconds the warm bright light surrounded them, and in the blink of an eye, they were back in David's bedroom.

A few minutes later, when the others were talking, Rocky became curious and went downstairs to the kitchen. When he got to the kitchen, he began walking around looking for something to eat. Mr.'s Skinner was also in the kitchen, getting some soda from the refrigerator. Rocky was walking across the floor, and Mr.'s Skinner accidentally stepped on his tale. The pain in Rockies' tail caused him to hiss so loud, Mr.'s Skinner could hear it! Rocky became visible for a short time. Mr.'s Skinner saw Rocky, and then he vanished! Mr.'s Skinner screamed and Mr. Skinner came running into the kitchen

"What's the matter?" Mr. Skinner asked.

"I just stepped on an orange cat and it vanished into thin air!" Mr.'s Skinner cried.

"Honey, I think you need a Psychiatrist." Mr. Skinner said.

"I don't need to see a doctor. I did see a cat!" Mr.'s Skinner exclaimed.

Mr.'s Skinners scream scared Rocky so badly, that he ran immediately upstairs.

"What is all the noise down there about?" David asked.

"Nothing at all." Rocky said.

"Come on Rocky, confess." Isaac said.

"OK, I was looking for some food, and David's mom stepped on my tail." Rocky replied.

"Look, if you guys want to stay here for tonight, you have to stay out of sight!" David exclaimed.

"He's right." Isaac replied.

In the meantime, back in the depths of Hell, the Dark One, and his worst demons were talking about what had taken place up to now. The Dark One spoke to his demons.

"Soon all of you will be released on the earth, to spread darkness."

"We spread darkness on the earth already." Spoke "Deceit."

"I know that you fool!" The Dark One shouted.

"I mean darker than ever before." The Dark One continued.

"How can that be?" "Hate" inquired.

"I will open up the portal to Hell, and release unheard of evil on the earth." The Dark One replied.

"You father will not permit that!" "Greed" exclaimed.

"I am planning to visit my father in the "Land of the Good." The Dark One said.

"He will not listen to you." "Hate" said.

"I will show him how worthless humans are, and then he will listen." The Dark One replied.

"Do you really think that you can change his mind about humans?" "Envy" asked.

"Yes, and once he is on our side, nothing in existence will stop us!" The Dark One exclaimed.

After hearing this, all of the Dark One's main demons began to laugh and cackle.

"The earth will finally be ours!" "Hate" exclaimed.

"Yes, we have millions of potential addicts." "Alcohol" said.

"King Addictions will be pleased." The Dark One said.

While the Dark One was planning to visit the Boss, his demon soldiers were celebrating their upcoming victory!

Back at the Skinner's house, Isaac was wondering when he was going to let David wear the spectacles, and how to prepare him for what he was going to see. The things, which David would see have never been seen by a human ever before! Isaac wondered if David could take the power of the spectacles and still keep his right mind. An order was an order, and the Boss had told him to let David wear the spectacles! Isaac decided to let David get some sleep before having him put on the spectacles.

In the "Land of the Good," the Boss knew of his son's visit, and was telling the other angels to stay clear of his son, while they were talking about the fate of the world.

Back in Hell, the Dark One was feeling confident about his father siding with him. He knew that once he told his father what he had to say, the Boss would change his mind and allow the destruction of the human world.

Chapter Seven

The Dark One Visits the "Land of the Good"

In the "Land of the Good," the Boss was spending time with some of his angels. He was in a part of Heaven, which had a beautiful landscape. It had green grass and blue skies. This part of Heaven also had deep blue lakes and fields of wheat. It was a very serene part of Heaven. While sitting on the bank of a lake, the Boss noticed that something was coming, he could feel that it was pure evil. The Boss knew that it had to be his dark son. Suddenly, he heard a loud thunderous voice coming from one of the fields of wheat,

"Father, look what you have done too me!" The voice exclaimed.

At that time there was a very large dark cloud coming in from the east of the land. The cloud had a face that was so hideous, that the other angels could not bear to look upon it. The face in the dark cloud had bright red eyes and blisters on its face. The face also had horns on its head, and very crooked sharp teeth. The angels began to fly off to escape the cloud; they all knew it was the Dark One!

"My face used to be so beautiful, and now it is hideous." The Dark One shouted.

As the cloud advanced, everything in its path began to wither and die. The wheat turned black and the waters became poisoned. The dark cloud brought with it death and destruction. The cloud moved its way up to the Boss, and then it stopped. The eyes in the cloud looked evil, but sad.

"Why do you torment me father?" The Dark One asked.

"You torment yourself." The Boss replied.

"You cast me out!" The Dark One exclaimed.

"Existence cast you out." The Boss replied.

"Why do you say that?" The Dark One asked.

"Existence will not tolerate darkness." The Boss said.

"Darkness is the only truth Father." The Dark One said.

"You are wrong Son." The Boss answered.

"The humans have found a new God, it is called money." The Dark One said.

"Money can buy only short lived happiness." The Boss replied.

"Money rules the human race." Spoke the Dark One.

"It is true; humans think that money can buy happiness." The Boss replied.

"They worship money more than they do you." The Dark One said.

"Not all of them do." The Boss replied.

"Most of them do, they are weak and pathetic and you should destroy them all." The Dark One said.

"They are still learning my Son." The Boss answered.

"Will you help me destroy them?" The Dark One asked.

"No." The Boss replied.

"Then I will return to my kingdom of Hell." The Dark One replied.

"Come to the light my Son!" The Boss exclaimed.

"I cannot. I am the darkness." The Dark One said.

The cloud with the face on it began to go back to where it came. While it was retreating, it said in a loud thunderous voice, "I know about the spectacles, and they will be mine!"

"I am the alpha and the omega. I have existed before time, and in the end only darkness will live." The Dark One concluded.

With his final words the Dark One tore a hole in time and headed back to Hell. He was getting ready to gather his dark forces together to find the Spectacles. The Dark One had almost had the spectacles, but that menacing spirit had stopped him! This time he would go to earth himself, and his strongest demons would go with him, and they would take human form!

After the Dark One left, the Boss gathered his angels and told them that they must help Isaac and his friends avoid being destroyed by the dark forces. He told them only one human will be allowed to see through the spectacles, and that would be David. The Boss further explained that he who wore the spectacles would be able to see all the way up to the end of time, and would have knowledge of whether the end will turn out good or bad. He told his angels that no other human being is to have this information, if the spectacles were to fall into the wrong hands, it would change the past and the future!

The angel Gabriel told the Boss that he and his other angels would help Isaac and David.

In Hell, the Dark One was speaking to his demons, and making plans to gain the spectacles.

"We know where the spirit Isaac is now. Why not go and get the spectacles! "Fear" shouted.

"We can't just break into the mortal world the way we appear." The Dark One said.

"Then we will possess some of the town people, and then get the spectacles!" "Hate" exclaimed.

"We must be careful, my Father is no fool!" The Dark One replied.

"Yes, he will try to stop us." "King Addictions" said.

"We do not want to start a war on Earth." "Deceit" replied.

"Why not?" "Confusion" asked.

"The humans must not know about an afterlife, it would give them hope." "Deceit" replied.

"Enough, we have much to do!" The Dark One shouted.

"As long as the humans do not see through the spectacles, they will continue to spread the word that God is dead!" "Greed" exclaimed.

"Yes, and you will become their new God. "Deceit" replied.

"We must not let the humans know there is any hope." The Dark One said.

While the other demons were talking, a shadow formed over all of them, and a foul smell came with the shadow. The other demons looked in the directions of the shadow and saw a thing with many heads shouting lies and blasphemies. The thing had no legs, and many different faces. The form had two huge arms, but no legs; it dragged itself along the base of Hell by its arms.

"Welcome "Insanity!" The Dark One exclaimed.

One of the heads began shouting, "Life has no meaning."

Another of the heads shouted, "You are spiritually weak, that is your problem."

Yet, another head shouted, "You need drugs and alcohol just to survive."

The thing stopped right in front of the Dark One, and

all of the heads looked at the creator of Hell. In unison, all of the heads shouted all at the same time, "Hail to death and misery!"

Behind "Insanity" "Death" followed, not the natural "Death," but, the unnatural "Death."

Unnatural "Death" always showed up when humans died unnatural deaths. He followed the demons: "War," "Hate," and "Murder," to name a few.

"Come "Insanity," we have many souls to steal." "Death" said.

It is true, many people died needlessly before their time, and that can only be called insane!

CHAPTER EIGHT
A VISIT TO THE NURSING HOME

BACK AT THE Skinner's house, Isaac, and his friends were talking about letting David put on "The Spectacles of Eternity."

"Should I put the spectacles on now?" David asked.

"The Boss says now is not the time to put the spectacles on." Isaac said.

"The Dark One knows about you now." Isaac continued.

"When will I get to put them on?" David asked.

"Soon." Isaac replied.

"For now we need to hide the spectacles for a day or two until we talk to the Boss." Sarah said.

"Where can we possibly hide them?" Whiskers asked.

"Yeah, the Dark One seems to know everything." Rocky said.

"I have an idea!" David exclaimed.

"What?" Isaac asked.

"We can let my Grandmother wear them." David replied.

"Where is your Grandmother?" Isaac asked.

"She lives at the Nursing Home in Town." Isaac replied.

David's Grandmother did live in a nursing facility in town. Her name was Beth. These days, Beth spent most of her time suffering from old age related sickness, and thinking about the days of her life, that flew by so fast. She kept her fond memories, and suffered in silence. Beth always had a kind word or a helping hand for many of the other residents, who lived at the nursing home. Beth was well loved by the Boss. The Boss had followed her entire life, and watched as she put aside her own troubles to help others who had worst problems. He was looking forward to meeting Beth in person. The Boss had one more thing that he wanted Beth to do before she was allowed to come home. He wanted her to see through the spectacles, and see what the future held for her. The Boss figured that he owed her this for all the help she gave to the sick and the poor.

"Let's go to the nursing home!" David exclaimed.

"None of the Dark One's demons will look there!" Sarah exclaimed.

So, the next day, off they went, David and the rest his friends headed for the nursing home. When they arrived, they went in through the employee's entrance. David's Grandmother lived on the Alzheimer's wing. The head nurse on the wing knew David from his previous visits. The nurse was a stout woman, with a loud voice. The nurse could not see the spirits with David, or the spectacles, which were being worn by Rocky.

"Hello David, have you come to see your Grandmother?" The nurse asked in a loud voice.

"I sure have Patty." David replied.

"Well, you just go on down to her room, she will be happy to see you." Patty said.

"I'm just glad she remembers who I am." David replied.

David walked down to his Grandmothers room, which

was 402, and knocked on the door, and went into the room. He found his Grandmother sitting on her bed crying.

"Grandma, why are you crying?" David asked.

Isaac and the others were sad to see her crying. "I just miss your Grandpa." Replied Beth, sadly.

"I know you do Grandma." David said.

"How have you been David?" Beth asked.

"Fine Grandma, I have some friends for you to meet." David said.

"I don't see anybody but you David." Beth replied.

"Take the spectacles and put them on your Grandma." Rocky said.

David took the spectacles from Rocky, the spectacles were invisible. David's Grandma did not understand why David wanted her to put on something, which she could not see. After talking to his Grandmother for awhile, David convince her to play along with him. David put the spectacles on his Grandma. Soon, Beth's eyes lit up, and she became amazed and very happy. Beth could now see Isaac, and Sarah, and their pets.

"My goodness!" Beth exclaimed.

"Can you see Isaac, and my other friends?" David asked.

"Yes, I see a pretty little girl!" Beth exclaimed.

"Thank you Beth." Sarah replied.

"Why can I see them now?" David's grandma asked.

"Because, you are wearing the spectacles." Isaac replied.

"How are the spectacles allowing me to see them?" Beth asked.

"My friend's are dead, they are spirits." David asked.

"Oh my!" Exclaimed Beth, fearfully.

"They are good spirits." David said.

"Well, that is ok then." Beth replied.

"It is nice to meet you Grandma Skinner." Isaac exclaimed.

"Thank you." Beth replied.

Beth's eyes were a clear green color. Her skin was old and wrinkled, but her eyes still had a youthful look. She asked David why he wanted her to meet his friends. David explained the situation, and told his Grandma they needed a place to hide the spectacles. Beth agreed to help them, but while she was talking to David, she saw a bright light, out of the light came her late husband. Beth began to cry with happiness.

The spirit of her husband walked up to Beth, and sat down next to her.

"Hi honey." Her late husband Robert said.

"Oh Robert, I have missed you so much!" Exclaimed Beth, sadly.

"I know honey." Robert replied.

"Life has been so lonely without you." Beth said.

"I have missed you to Beth." Robert said.

"Can you stay awhile?" Beth asked.

"No, it is not allowed right now." Robert replied.

"Why not?" Beth asked.

"I am a spirit, we are not allowed back into this world after death." Robert answered.

"When will I see you again Robert?" Beth asked.

"Soon." Robert said.

"Will we stay together then?" Beth asked.

"Yes, then we will be together forever." Robert Replied.

Robert began to walk back into the light, but before he was all the way into the light, he turned and said, "Hold on to the precious memories of our life together Beth."

"I will Robert, I will, I promise." Beth replied.

"We have to leave now Grandma." David said.

"We will be back for the spectacles in two days." Isaac added.

"Ok, I'll see you in two days." Beth replied.

David and his friends left the nursing home and headed back to the Skinner's house. On the way back to the skinner's house, Whiskers saw another cat on a street in David's neighborhood. Forgetting that he was a spirit, whiskers took off after the cat.

"Quick, stop him!" Isaac exclaimed.

"Whiskers, come back right now!" Sarah shouted.

Whiskers liked Sarah, and when he heard her voice, he stopped and came back.

"What do we do now?" David asked.

"We go back to your place and wait." Rocky replied.

"Won't they find us there?" Sarah asked.

"The Dark One can feel when the spectacles are near." Said Isaac

"Then maybe we should not go to David's house." Sarah said.

"Where else could we go?" Whiskers asked.

"We could stay at my friend's house in Muncie for a few days." David said.

"I have a better idea David." Isaac said.

"What?" Sarah asked.

"We could sail on the "Sea of Serenity" for a couple of days." Isaac replied.

"I could tell my parent's I'm going to stay a couple of days with a school buddy." David said.

"That would work." Isaac replied.

So, off they went to the Skinner's house. David intended to tell his mother and father that he was going to spend some time at a friend's house.

In the mean time, back at the Skinner's house, the phone rings.

"I'll get it honey." Mr.'s Skinner said.

Mr.'s Skinner answered the phone, and after a minute or two, angrily hung the phone up.

"What's the matter honey?" Mr. Skinner asked.

"Someone on the phone just told me to give up the spectacles, or he would lay our soul's to waste." Mr.'s Skinner replied.

"You would think that the kids in this town could think of something better than prank phone calls." Mr. Skinner replied.

"He said he was the Dark One." Mr.'s Skinner said.

"More like the dumb one!" Mr. Skinner replied.

What the Skinner's did not know, was that it was the Dark One trying to scare them into finding out about the spectacles, and who had them? The Dark One was having some problems pin pointing the spectacles, because Isaac was making sure the spectacles kept moving from one place to the other.

The Dark One decided to send "Fear," along with "Deceit" to earth to find the spectacles, and bring them to him. They would first, go to earth as spirits, and then possess two of the town folks to do their bidding!

Once David arrived at his home, he talked to his parent's about staying over a couple nights with one of his school buddy's. After telling David about, what Mr. Skinner thought to be a prank phone call, David's parents gave him the go ahead. David told his parent's that his friend's phone was not working, and he would try to call them from a pay phone. David had always been honest in the past, so his parents trusted him to stay with a friend. Isaac suggested that they go to the graveyard, and leave on the trip from there. David agreed.

As David and his friends were heading for the graveyard, "Fear," and "Deceit", were already in the town of Santa Claus Indiana, looking for victims. They expected everything to go smooth.

CHAPTER NINE
FEAR AND DECEIT FIND VICTIMS

IN THE FORM of spirits, "Deceit," and "Fear," floated through the town of Santa Claus, looking for victims to possess. They decided to stop in a tavern to look for humans. They both floated in through the front door of the tavern and heard music playing and the sound of merriment. "Deceit" found his victim. His victims name was Delbert Sound. Delbert was a truck driver, who had an overnight stay in Santa Claus, after he had dropped off his load of new cars to an automotive dealer ship. Delbert was a large man, with brown hair and green eyes. He stood six feet, five inches tall, and had a mustache and bushy beard. He also had a huge beer gut. "Deceit" floated into Delbert's beer glass, in order to get inside of Delbert and possess him. Delbert took one drink of the beer and "Deceit" possessed him! Delbert's eyes turned dark red, and Delbert began dancing around the tavern shouting.

"Hey everyone, they should have named this place Satan Claus Indiana."

Now it was time for "Fear" to make his move. He found one of the regular visitors of the tavern, Bob Baker. Bob was already on his way to being totally drunk. "Fear" simply floated into his bottle of beer, and Bob drank it. Bob stood straight up out of his seat and started to walk up to the bar. Bob was a thin man with grey hair and sharp blue eyes, he was about five foot, nine inches, and had been drunk most of his adult life.

When Bob got near the bar, the bartender asked, "You want another drink Bob?"

"No, I'm giving drinking up for good!" Bob exclaimed.

When he heard what Bob said, the bartender almost had a heart attack. The words that came out of Bob's mouth shocked the bartender.

"You feel alright Bob?" The bar tender asked.

"I have never felt better in my life!" Bob exclaimed.

Of course it was not Bob talking; it was the spirit "Fear."

"I have more important things to do than drink." Bob said.

Delbert stopped dancing and look at Bob.

"Come on, we have work to do!" Delbert exclaimed.

The first place that Bob and Delbert went to was the Skinner's house. They walked down the main street in Santa Claus Indiana, until they came to the edge of town, and they headed into the woods towards David's house.

In the meantime, David, Isaac, and Sarah, along with Whiskers and Rocky, were at the graveyard. They were standing by Sarah's grave. Isaac told everyone to stand in a circle. When everyone was in a circle, Isaac brought the warm white light and they all vanished. When the light faded they were in a ship on the "Sea of Serenity."

After walking awhile, Delbert spotted David's house.

"There it is!" Delbert exclaimed.

"Come on, let's go see if that kid David, and his spirit friend are there." Bob replied.

"The two demons, who had possessed the human bodies,

headed for the front porch of the house. When they got on the porch, they looked in the window and saw Mr. and Mr.'s Skinner sitting in the living room, watching television.

The Demons knocked on the door. Mr. Skinner answered the door.

"Hello sir, my name is Bob." "Fear" said.

"Can I help you with something?" Mr. Skinner asked.

"We are looking for a young man named David." Bob replied.

"He's staying with a friend for a couple of days." Mr. Skinner replied.

"What do you want my son for?" Mr. Skinner asked.

"Where does his friend live?" Bob inquired.

"That is none of your business!" Mr. Skinner exclaimed.

"Tell me where he's at, or we will turn your soul over to the Dark One." Delbert said.

"That is it, I'm calling the police!" Exclaimed Mr. Skinner, angrily.

"No need for that sir, this is a small town and we will find him." Bob said.

At that time, Bob and Delbert headed back down the sidewalk, away from the Skinner's house.

Mr. Skinner called the police to report these two men, who were looking for his son. He did not like the looks of either of them, and was fearful for David.

On the "Sea of Serenity," David was looking out onto the peaceful and quiet sea. Everything on the sea was always calm and peaceful.

"I wish that we could stay here forever!" David exclaimed.

"Me too." Sarah replied.

"We still have a mission to complete." Isaac said.

So, David and Isaac, and friends, sat peacefully on board the ship, taking it easy.

Back in the town of Santa Claus, Bob and Delbert had just gotten a message from the Dark One.

The Dark One told them to seek the spectacles out at the nursing facility, which the boy, David's Grandmother was staying. He also told them that she had the spectacles, and that she was hiding them for the boy David and his spirit friends. The Dark One told the two demons to get the spectacles no matter what! Even if they had to take the life of the boy's grandmother!

Well, as you can guess, the two demons headed off for the nursing home to get the spectacles. They were not sure where it was located, so they knew they would have to stop and ask someone. They were now, in town on foot, and spotted a gas station. They went up to the station and walked inside. Before asking the clerk for directions, Delbert became hungry, and was looking around for a Twinkie. He found the Twinkies and began eating them, and throwing the wrappers on the floor. When the clerk saw Delbert eating the Twinkies, he shouted at him, "Hey buddy, you going to pay for those?"

Bob looked at the clerk, and asked, "What you going to do about it punk?"

"I am going to call the police." The clerk answered.

At that point, Bob started changing into his demon form. His body grew to ten feet, and his teeth and fingernails began to get longer. Large horns grew out of his head, and his body turned the color of red. Soon smoke was coming from Bob's nostrils. He then looked at the clerk and said,

"I said what you going to do about it?" The demon asked.

Upon seeing this, the clerk let out a scream, and hid below the counter. The demon was having fun, and decided to harass the clerk some more. The demon "Fear," walked up to the counter. His feet were hoof like and he had huge arms and legs. The demon tore the counter out from the floor, and found the clerk kneeling down and scared to death. The demon then picked the clerk up off the floor, and brought him up to his teeth.

"You would taste very good right now!" exclaimed the demon.

"Please, I beg you not to kill me!" The clerk shouted.

The demon began to laugh loudly and started swinging the clerk back and forth by his head.

The demon put the clerk down, and took the form of Bob again.

"Do you still want us to pay for this?" asked Bob.

"Just take is and leave!" The clerk exclaimed.

"We will be glad to leave, as soon as you tell us how to get to the towns nursing home." said Bob.

The clerk took out a map of the town and showed Bob that the nursing home was about four blocks up the main street. The clerk also told the two demons that the name of the nursing home was Quiet Meadows, and it was the only nursing home in town.

"Thanks." said Delbert.

Both men left the store laughing at the clerk.

At the nursing home, nobody had any idea that they would be visited by these two demons. Beth had no idea that they would be after her for the spectacles!

Delbert had heard earlier that there was an amusement park close by and decided that he and Bob could stop by the park and have some fun. The Dark One would have been very angry to know that Delbert and Bob were wasting time getting the spectacles.

Delbert told Bob that it would be fun to go to the Ferris wheel and make it go in reverse to scare the customers riding on it. Bob agreed and they headed for the Ferris wheel. When they arrived at the Ferris wheel, they stood and watched for awhile. Then Delbert raised his hand and pointed at the Ferris wheel, the Ferris wheel stopped and started again in reverse! The people on the Ferris wheel began to scream in horror! And Bob and Delbert began laughing loudly.

"Look at them scream, this is so much fun!" exclaimed Delbert.

"It is fun." replied Bob.

As the two of them were laughing, a cell phone began ringing in Delbert's pocket. Delbert reached into his pocket and took out the cell phone.

"What is that?" asked Bob.

"Looks like some kind of telephone." replied Delbert.

"Well, answer it fool!" screamed Bob.

Delbert answered the phone, and in a second or two seemed to become very fearful.

"What is wrong with you?" asked "Fear."

"It's the Dark One and he wants to talk to you." replied "Deceit".

Delbert handed Bob the phone.

"Hello, Yes.....but.....I understand oh Dark One." said Bob, who was trembling with fear.

Bob ended the call.

"You are an idiot Delbert!" Bob screamed.

"What did I do wrong?" asked Delbert.

"We are supposed to be getting the spectacles, not play-ing games!" Bob shouted.

"The Dark One is very angry and we don't want him coming to earth to deal with us." Bob continued.

"You are right, let's get out of here and go to the nursing home." replied Delbert.

"The fear the Dark One causes is worse than me, and I am "Fear!" exclaimed Bob.

The two demons in human bodies headed off for the nursing home. On the way they decided they wanted to drive, so they took the form of demons and flagged down a car. When the driver saw the two demons, he was scared to death, and left the car running for his life. Delbert and Bob went back to their human forms and drove off in the car laughing. Deep down inside, they both knew it was not a laughing matter, if they did not get the spectacles soon, they would have to face punishment from the Dark One!

CHAPTER TEN
HELL COMES TO THE NURSING HOME

WHEN DELBERT AND Bob arrived at the nursing home, they sat in the car out in the parking lot to discuss how they were going to go about getting the spectacles. They decided that going to the front desk might cause suspicion, so they were going to use a back door to the nursing home. What they did not know, was that the back door they were going to use would take them straight in to the Alzheimer's unit!

Inside the nursing home, in the Alzheimer's unit, sitting in her wheel chair by the back door, was a patient named Wanda. She was suffering from a really bad case of Alzheimer's, and was also blind. Wanda had no idea that she was soon going to be confronted by Delbert and Bob. When Delbert and Bob walked into the back door, the first person they saw was Wanda.

"Hello." Delbert said.

"Hello." Wanda replied.

"We were looking for a Beth Skinner; do you know what room she's in?" Bob asked.

"Sure I do!" Wanda exclaimed.

"What room?" Bob inquired.

"What room for what?" Wanda asked.

69

"I'm looking for Beth Skinner's room." Bob asked, for the second time.

"If you want the best dinner, you don't have to eat it on the moon." Wanda replied.

Delbert and Bob were becoming very upset.

"Where is her room at grandma?" Delbert asked.

"What room?" Wanda asked.

"This woman is messing with us!" Bob exclaimed, angrily.

"Why don't we show her what we really look like?" Delbert said.

"Yeah, lets' change into our demon bodies." Bob replied.

Bob and Delbert transformed into their demon selves, and they looked hideous. Delbert turned into a tall and lanky figure, with horns and deep red eye's. Delbert was now "Deceit", in person. Bob also transformed, and was now the hideous figure of "Fear." Both of the demons were over ten feet tall, and smell of death and disease. Hovering over Wanda, "Deceit" put his green lanky hands on Wanda, and said, "I bet you will tell us what room Beth Skinner is in now, won't you?"

Well, of course, Wanda was blind, and could not see either one of the demons.

"Boy, it sure got hot in here!" exclaimed Wanda.

"Fool, tell us where she is, or we will tear you apart!" "Deceit" shouted.

"Tell you where who is?" Wanda asked.

By now, both "Deceit" and "Fear" were very angry and frustrated.

"Let's kill her!" said "Deceit".

"Let's just leave; this situation is more confusing than being in Hell!" Bob exclaimed.

When Bob and Delbert took on their human form

and left Wanda sitting there, they were so confused; they didn't know what to do next. When Bob and Delbert were off looking for Beth, the Boss appeared, and stood next to Wanda. The Boss bent over and hugged Wanda, and then whispered in her ear, "Wanda, you did a good job with those two demons."

Wanda smiled.

The Boss whispered in her ear again. He told her soon she would be done with all of her suffering and misery, and after she went to sleep, she would wake up in the "Land of the Good." He also told her that when she woke up, she would be young again. Wanda continued smiling.

"When you wake up, you will be able to see and think clearly, and there will be no more sadness or pain, only happiness." said the Boss.

"You have done the best you could in this life and treated people kind, and now it is you're turn to be happy and to be treated kind." continued the Boss.

"I am afraid to die." Wanda said, who was crying now.

"Do not be afraid, I will be there to help you through it." Said the Boss.

Wanda began to smile again. The Boss told her that when she arrived at her new home there would be no more tears, only joy.

In the meantime, Bob and Delbert were walking through the nursing home looking for Beth.

They finally gave up and went to the front desk and scared the front desk nurse in to telling them what room Beth was in.

"It's about time we found her room number!" exclaimed Bob.

"Yeah, come on lets go get the spectacles." Delbert replied.

Beth still had the spectacles on her face and could see

many wonderful things. When the two demons broke into her room, she could see that they were not human and not good spirits!

"Alright lady, give us the spectacles!" Delbert shouted.

"I can't do that." Beth replied.

"Good, let's take her life now." Bob said.

"Why can't you just give them to us?" Delbert asked.

"Because he is going to give them to you." Beth replied.

At that moment, the room filled up with light, and the Boss walked out of the light and looked at Bob and Delbert.

"Hello boys, good to see you again!" The Boss exclaimed.

A look of dread came over the faces of Bob and Delbert, who were really "Fear" and "Deceit".

"You have no business here!" "Fear" exclaimed.

"Be gone or the Dark One will destroy you!" "Deceit" shouted.

"Say boys, there are a lot of angels in the "Land of the Good," who would like to see you." The Boss said.

The two demons could not see the form the Boss came in, because the light was blinding them.

"No thanks!" "Deceit" exclaimed.

"Leave now, or I call on the Dark One." "Fear" said.

"It's time for you boys to go back to Hell." The Boss said.

The Boss raised his hands and told the demons to be gone. Knowing the Boss was much more powerful; they let out an agonizing scream and departed the human bodies. The Boss walked up to Beth and said, "You are safe now Beth."

Bob and Delbert woke up and shook their heads. Bob looked at Delbert and said.

"I don't know where we are, but it sure isn't the bar."

"Come on let's get out of here and go have a beer." Delbert replied.

The two men left the nursing home thinking they had just woke up from a drunken black out.

"Oh, thank you so much." Beth said, in a relieved voice.

The Boss told Beth that soon she would be with him, in the "Land of the Good." The Boss told Beth to hang on to the spectacles, because David and Isaac would be picking them up soon. The Boss, then spoke to Isaac's soul and told him to get back to this world, and get the spectacles from Beth.

In another world, Isaac was talking to Sarah, when he heard the Boss's message.

"Come on, we have to get back to the world of humans!" Isaac exclaimed.

"Why do we have to leave?" David said.

"The Boss wants us to go back and pick up the spectacles." Isaac replied. So, once again, David, Isaac, Sarah, Whiskers, and Rocky headed back to get the spectacles from Beth.

When they arrived at the Nursing Home, Beth gave them the spectacles, and bid them goodbye.

David did not know at the time, he was never going to see Beth on this earth again. David, Isaac, and their friends headed for the graveyard, where Isaac was going to have David put the spectacles on. When they were on the way to the graveyard, everything grew very quiet. They could hear no noise at all. The wind stopped blowing and the people of the town stopped moving! It was as if someone had turned off a light switch, and stopped life. David became scared.

"What is going on?" David asked nervously.

"I think the Dark One is coming up from Hell to get the spectacles himself!" Isaac exclaimed.

Suddenly, the ground shook, and a loud voice echoed through the quiet town of Santa Claus.

"You dare defy me!" The Dark One shouted.

"You have no business here." Isaac shouted.

"Give me the spectacles now, or I will destroy all of you." The Dark One shouted.

"No." Isaac replied.

Suddenly, a huge shadow filled the town of Santa Claus. David and his friends felt death and decay, and everything bad. The shadow became so dark, Isaac could not see any of his other friends.

"Help me!" a shout came in the darkness. Isaac knew that it was David's voice. The Dark One did not know that Isaac had the spectacles. After Isaac heard the cry, everything went back to normal. It was daylight again, the wind was blowing, and the town was alive again. When the darkness cleared Isaac looked around and saw all of his friends, except David! Isaac was afraid that the Dark One would take David to the deepest part of Hell. Isaac had to devise a plan to get David back!

When the darkness cleared, David was standing in front of the Dark One. The Dark One was in the form of a giant demon. The demon's body was blood red. Its head had huge horns on it. The Dark One had long arms, with claw like hands. The fingernails on the demons hands were very long, and sharp. Fire and smoke came out of The Dark Ones mouth as he spoke.

"Give me the spectacles boy!" The Dark One shouted.

"I don't have them." David replied.

"Who has the spectacles?" The Dark One asked.

"I don't know." David replied.

The Dark One let out a shout. The shout was so loud that

it shook the foundation of Hell. Surrounding David were millions of souls in misery. The souls were being tortured by demons. David was surrounded by mountains of fire. The landscape was charred and black. David had the feeling of decay all around him. It was as if his worst nightmares had come to life!

"Welcome to your new home boy!" The Dark One shouted.

"I told you that I don't have the spectacles." David shouted.

"Maybe some time in Hell will refresh your memory." The Dark One said.

David was really scared; he thought that he would be in Hell forever.

"I must go and find the spectacles, enjoy my home!" The Dark One exclaimed.

The Dark One began laughing loudly, and then he turned into smoke and was gone. David found the first cave that he could find and hid in it. The Dark One figured he knew who had the spectacles.

"If David did not have the spectacles, Isaac would." The Dark One thought to himself.

Back on earth, Isaac and Sarah, along with Whiskers and Rocky were making plans on how to get David out of Hell. They knew the Dark One would figure out who really had the spectacles. Isaac knew they had to work fast! To stay safe, Isaac took his friends to the "Sea of Serenity." He knew the Dark One would never show up there. The Dark One, hated serenity! The Dark One knew that the spectacles must not fall into human hands, but it was more of a nagging feeling than anything. He did not know the reason to keep the spectacles out of human hands, but he felt that it would be the end of him if he allowed humans to have the knowledge that the spectacles held. The Dark One felt so strongly about the spectacles, that he was willing to wage war with Heaven to get them! The Dark One knew that the Boss had forbidden him to ever go to the "Sea of Serenity." After thinking about it for awhile, the Dark One decided the only way to get what he wanted was to declare war! So he sent a demon to heaven with a message to his father. The message stated that Hell had declared war on Heaven and they would destroy Heaven, and everything in it.

When the Boss received the message, he immediately called a meeting of the head angels. The Boss had them meet with him in the highest court in Heaven. The Boss always liked the way the Romans constructed their Courts, so that is the way the high court of the Boss appeared. The Boss was in the middle of the building at a podium, and the head angels were seated in a circle around him. The building was made of white stone, and resembled a building built in the days of the Roman Empire.

Chapter Eleven
The Court of Heaven Votes

THE TALK AMONG the angels was noisy and intense. Gabriel had already put on his armor, and his sword. The angel Saul had done the same.

"Quiet please!" The Boss shouted.

"By now you all know that Hell has declared war on us." The Boss continued.

The Boss appeared as an old man with white hair and blue eyes. The robe he had on was also white, and long.

"If it's war they want, lets' give it to them!" Gabriel shouted.

Gabriel was a muscular angel. He had golden hair, and fire in his eyes. Gabriel was use to war, the Boss had sent him on many past missions to destroy certain enemies.

"We will drive them back into the depths of Hell where they belong!" Saul shouted.

"Why are you always so quick to choose violence Saul?" The Boss asked.

"We have no choice; it's them, or us." Saul answered.

There were five hundred of the Bosses top angels in the courtroom.

"We shall take a vote!" The boss exclaimed.

The boss then had Gabriel pass out paper and pencils to all the angels.

"Vote yes or no for war." The Boss shouted.

The courtroom became very quiet, and the sound of papers and pencils could be heard among the angels. While the angels were voting, the Boss sat down to take a break. Suddenly, a bright yellow light appeared in front of the Boss.

"Hello Athena." The Boss said.

"You know my name is not Athena." The angel who just appeared said.

"I know, but every since you appeared to those Roman soldiers and they gave you a name, I've used it." The Boss said.

If I'm the goddess of wisdom, then I will tell you that war is not wise." The angel spoke.

The angel's real name was Angela. The Boss got a kick out of calling her Athena.

"I know Angela, but my son is forcing it on me." The Boss said.

"You don't have to fight." Angela said.

"If we do not fight he will destroy us!" The boss exclaimed.

"Is there no way out of it?" Angela asked.

"There is no way that I can think of." The Boss replied.

While talking to Angela, Gabriel informed the Boss that all of the votes had been cast. The Boss told Angela that he would speak with her later, and Angela took the form of a yellow light, and was gone. The Boss went to the podium, and counted the votes. After counting the votes, he shouted,

"The votes have been cast, and they say that we go to war!"

After getting the results of the voting, Gabriel flew off to get his troops ready for the war with Hell. In the meantime the Dark One was gathering his troops in Hell. In the deepest part of Hell, The Dark One stood on a mountain of fire to address his troops.

"Look at us, we were once angels!" The Dark One shouted.

"My father has done this to us!" The Dark One continued.

"We want war!" "Ignorance" shouted.

"Dawn your armor and prepare for war!" The Dark One shouted.

The deepest bowels of Hell were awake. All of the demons were gathering their best weapons, and preparing for battle. The Dark One told his army of demons that he was going to take back heaven and cast its entire people into Hell. Back in Heaven thousands of angels with golden armor and swords, were flying through the skies of Heaven heading in every different direction to defend Heaven.

Meanwhile, on the "Sea of Serenity," Isaac received word from an angel of the upcoming war.

"This might be our chance to free David!" Isaac exclaimed.

"Why is now a good time?" Sarah asked.

"Because of the confusion in Hell, we could sneak in and get David." Isaac replied.

"How do we get into Hell?" Sarah asked.

"We go to the castle of "King Addictions," and climb down the bottomless pit in the lower part of what used to be his castle." Isaac replied.

"We can't use our powers there!" Sarah exclaimed.

"We will have to find rope, and climb down into Hell." Isaac replied.

"What about the keys to the gates of Hell?" Sarah asked.

"We will have to steal them from the gate keeper." Isaac answered.

"But the gate keeper is "Insanity." Sarah exclaimed.

"I know it won't be easy, but we have to save David." Isaac replied.

"You need a plan to defeat "Insanity." Whiskers said.

"Yes, he is one of the most evil demons from Hell." Rocky said.

"Then we will come up with a plan, in the meantime, turn this ship around and head for what used to be the dark side of "Nowhere Land." Isaac said.

As David was hiding in a cave in Hell, he began seeing demons in armor marching past the cave he was in. At first he thought they were looking for him, but, then he noticed they were heading towards huge gates. The gates were on the top of a very high mountain of fire. After awhile, David was relieved to see that the demons were not even paying attention to him. The demons appeared to be marching off to some kind of war! At first he thought it would be a good time to try to find a way out of Hell; however, after further thought he decided not to move. David could see that there were too many demons outside of the cave to even try to escape! So, he continued to wait, in hopes of help coming soon to get him out of Hell.

The Boss was back in Heaven still trying to find a way for a peaceful solution. He did not think that war would accomplish anything; and it bothered him greatly that he could think of no other solutions. The angel Gabriel had the armies of Heaven in place and was ready for battle. The Boss decided there was no other way out. He would have to fight a war with his son. After all, he had tried to think of every other possible way out of war. The Court of Heaven had made the decision in favor of war; therefore, he would go along with it. If anything came to his mind during this time of sadness, he would stop the war and use another means to deal with his son. The Boss kept wandering if he should order another court session and take another vote. He had no doubt that Gabriel and his armies would defeat his son, but he still held the belief that war was good for nothing, and that everyone involved in a war loses. With just a little more time, he could have David put on the spectacles and see what the Boss was trying to get him to see. After David wore the spectacles; the Boss could banish the spectacles in some remote world, and after a time, they would be forgotten! The Boss knew that if David wore the spectacles, he would spread the word to many other people. The Boss needed people to start paying more attention to him again, and quit putting material things before him. Once the word got out about what David saw, people would start thinking more about God, and his son would see that people can change back to believing in a higher power other then themselves. The Boss knew that too much greed and want existed on the planet, and he knew it was because many people were blaming him for wars and other bad things, and shutting him out of their life. The Boss also knew that he did not start wars; it was people using his name to start wars. It was not the Boss starting wars, it was people! Nothing bad came from the Boss; only good. Bad came from the Dark One, but the Boss knew that earth was in-between Heaven and Hell. The earth was full of bad things and good things.

CHAPTER TWELVE:
GOING TO KING ADDICTION'S CASTLE

I SAAC SAILED THE ship from the "Sea of Eternity," to what used to be the dark side of "Nowhere Land." After docking the ship, Isaac, Sarah, Whiskers, and Rocky headed for the Castle that used to belong to "King Addictions." Isaac knew that once he and his friends scaled the wall to the end of the bottomless pit, he would have to find a way to get the keys to Hell from "Insanity." First he would have to take all of the rope, which he had on the ship and tie it together. He had no idea how far down he and his sister would have to go, but he had to try! Whiskers and Rocky were getting scared. They knew it wasn't called the bottomless pit for nothing!

"Insanity" received word from the Dark One that Isaac would try to rescue his friend David. He told "Insanity" to be on his guard, and if he saw them, he was to cast them into the dungeon of lost souls. "Insanity" told the Dark One that he would love to destroy them!

One of "Insanity's" heads began to laugh. Another of his heads spoke,

"Yes, oh yes I want to kill them master!"

Yet another one of "Insanity's" heads spoke and out of his mouth came words of evil and death, and his breath, if brought to earth, would kill any human within a mile of him!" Since, "Insanity" had no legs; he dragged himself across the bowels of Hell with his huge arms. The sight of him caused the other demons in Hell to hide in fear.

In the meantime Isaac had put together enough rope to get started with the climb down the pit. Sarah told Whiskers and Rocky to be strong. Finally, after walking awhile, Isaac and Sarah found the castle. They went in through the front door. The front door was a huge wooden door with black metal handles. Once into the castle they headed for the bottom floor of the castle. After looking around for awhile they heard a sound, as if many people were wailing in misery. The sound led them to the room where the bottomless pit was!

"I feel sorry for all those poor people!" Sarah exclaimed.

"I know Sarah, but we have to save David!" Isaac exclaimed.

Isaac tied the rope to a stone chair that was in the room, and threw the rope down into the bottomless pit. Isaac knew the rope would not be long enough; however, if the rope took them down far enough, they may be able to drop the rest of the way to the entrance to Hell. Isaac took one of the torches from the wall and lit it with a stick match he had found.

"Come on, lets' get going!" Isaac exclaimed."

Isaac went first; he climbed over the wall surrounding the bottomless pit and lowered himself down into it. He held the torch in his left hand, and climbed with his right hand. After he was down a few feet, Sarah climbed up over the wall and lower her-self into the pit. Whiskers and Rocky followed Sarah down into the pit. After climbing down for a few minutes, Isaac could smell a foul odor, and hear wailing and crying. He knew he was getting closer to the gates of Hell. After going down farther, Isaac could see light. The light appeared to be coming from torches at the bottom of the pit. Isaac let go of the rope, and fell the rest of the way to Hell. Isaac felt relief that he had put together enough rope to get him close enough to drop the rest of the way to the bottom. Once he reached the bottom, he waited for Sarah, and Whiskers and Rocky. When they were all at the bottom of the pit all they saw at first, were torches on the wall. They also saw many hallways. Not knowing which of the hallways to take, they just picked one and headed through it. After walking awhile, the odor, which, Isaac smelled earlier, became stronger. The sounds of wailing and crying became louder. As soon as Isaac and Sarah walked out of the hallway, a huge hand grabbed Sarah. Sarah screamed in fear. Just as Isaac turned to see what had happened, another hand grabbed him. "Insanity" had captured both of them!

"Now you will go to the dungeon of lost souls for-ever!" One of "Insanity's" faces exclaimed. Another one of "Insanity's" faces said, "You will be lost forever!"

"Insanity" began dragging himself across the floor of Hell towards the dungeon of lost souls. Isaac tried to break free, but, "Insanity's" arms were too strong. Sarah was shouting at "Insanity," to let them go. Whiskers and Rocky hid inside one of the hallways of Hell.

"We have to save them!" Whiskers exclaimed.

"Forget it." Rocky replied.

"Why?" Whiskers asked.

"It's better to be a live chicken than a dead duck!" Rocky replied.

"I'm going to help them, if you want to stay in Hell by yourself, go ahead." Whiskers said.

"I changed my mind!" Rocky exclaimed.

Whiskers knew that "Insanity" was aware that the two animal spirits were there, but, did not consider them that important. Whiskers decided the only way to help Isaac and Sarah, was to attack "Insanity!"

"You're going to do what?" Rocky shouted.

"I'm going to attack "Insanity." Whiskers replied.

"I think "Insanity" is rubbing off on you." Rocky said.

"We need to stop him before he reaches the dungeon of lost souls." Whiskers said.

"If we are going to be destroyed, let's get it over with." Rocky said.

So, Whiskers and Rocky left the hallway and started quietly following "Insanity."

After awhile, "Insanity" sensed that he was being followed. He decided to crush the two animal spirits with one of his arms! "Insanity" turned around quickly to surprise Whiskers and Rocky, as he turned he saw a black and orange piece of fur flying at his faces

Whiskers and Rocky got a running start and outright attacked! They ran and jumped towards "Insanity." Whiskers landed on one of "Insanity's" faces, and Rocky landed, clawing on to one of the other faces. "Insanity" was surprised, and went to grab Whiskers and Rocky from his faces. While he was doing that, he forgot about Isaac and Sarah, and let go of them. They were free! After picking themselves up off the floor, they looked to see what was going on. They saw Whiskers and Rocky clawing at "Insanity," and they saw "Insanity's" large hands trying to grab them, and pull them off.

"We need to save them!" Sarah shouted.

"I know." Isaac replied.

Isaac looked around, until he found a cliff. He walked over and looked down, and saw that the drop off the cliff went at least a mile down, and at the bottom was a lake of fire! Whiskers and Rocky were now in "Insanity's" grip. "Insanity" threw them off his faces, and they hit the ground, but not until Whiskers and Rocky scratched two of his faces up pretty bad! "Insanity" had another face, but it was busy making sure that Whiskers and Rocky were not attacking again. When whiskers got up off the ground, he looked at Isaac, as if to say, "what do I do next?"

Isaac looked at Whiskers, and then pointed to the key on "Insanity's" belt. Whiskers got the idea. Isaac wanted Whiskers to jump up and take the key to the gates of Hell from "Insanity."

"Hey ugly, you can't even win a fight with a dog and cat!" Isaac shouted.

"Insanity" saw Isaac and started pushing himself towards Isaac with his huge arms. "Insanity" was very angry and was dragging himself fast! Isaac stood at the face of the cliff waiting for "Insanity." At exactly the right moment, Isaac stepped aside, and "Insanity" fell of the cliff! But, not before Whiskers snatched the keys from his belt!

"Good job Whiskers!" Isaac shouted.

"Thanks for not saying good dog." Whiskers replied.

Isaac got the keys from Whiskers and they all went to the gate and put the key into the lock. After the key was turned, the gates to Hell opened! Isaac and Sarah, along with Whiskers and Rocky, went through the gate. The crying of the souls in torment was getting louder. After they walked about a mile, they came to an old stone stairway; which, winded its' way farther down into the depths of Hell. They started their climb downward. Along the way they saw many demons torturing souls. The demons were so busy at their job, Isaac, along with his sister and friends, went unnoticed. Farther down they went, until they had to stop and hide. They hid behind some rocks they had found. As they were hiding, they could see the soldiers of Hell marching past, heading for the gates of Hell. Isaac figured they would go through the gates and fly up and out of the bottomless pit. After they got out of the pit, they would make their way out of "Nowhere Land," and fly up towards

Heaven, where they would do battle with the angels. After the demons had marched past Isaac, he grabbed his sister's hand and said,

"Come on, we need to get going!"

Sarah took Isaac's hand, and they headed even farther into the depths of Hell. Along the way they saw a man who was very bloody and had many wounds on his body.

"Who are you?" Isaac asked.

"I am a tortured soul." The man replied.

"Why are you tortured?" Sarah asked.

"I am tortured by the demons who work for "Hate." The man replied.

Sarah went to the man and put her arms around him.

"You don't have to hate anymore, let go of the pain." Sarah said.

All of a sudden the man began to cry, and he let go of the hate that had imprisoned him for his whole life, and for all of the years he was in Hell. His torn up body became encircled in a white light and his soul was released. His soul floated out of Hell and up towards Heaven. After the soul had been set free, Sarah took hold of Isaac's hand and they continued looking for David.

David was still in the cave trying to figure out how he was going to get out of Hell. He looked outside of the cave and noticed that the soldiers had passed. David walked out of the cave and looked around. As smoke and fire continued to roar in the pit of Hell he had been taken to, he could see four shapes walking out of the smoke. As the shapes came closer, he realized it was Isaac, Sarah, and Whiskers and Rocky. He was so happy to see them he just started shouting at them!

"Isaac!" David shouted.

Sarah thought she heard a voice shouting. She stopped Isaac and looked at him, and said,

"Do you hear that?"

"Hear what?" Isaac asked.

"Don't you hear the shouting?" Sarah asked

Isaac listened harder, and then he heard it to!

"David, is that you?" Isaac shouted.

David heard Isaac and began running towards him, Sarah saw David coming towards them at a distance and pointed David out to Isaac. When David reached them, he hugged Isaac, and then Sarah, and told them how glad he was to see them.

"I thought my life was over." David said to Isaac.

"I am so happy we found you!" Isaac said, with a sigh of relief.

"We have to leave before the Dark One finds out we are here." Sarah said.

"She's right David, lets' go." Isaac said.

"Yeah, lets' get out of here." David replied.

David and his friends headed back to the gates of Hell. After walking awhile, they reached the gates and went through them. Isaac led them all back to the exit of the bottomless pit, and was able to reach the rope, and climb back up into the castle of "King Addictions." David and the others followed Isaac, and soon they were all back in the castle.

"Where do we go from here?" David asked.

"We need to get to the ship and back out onto the sea." Isaac said.

Once on board the ship they set sail. After sailing on the "Sea of Serenity" for awhile, Isaac turned to his friends and said, "Now that we are out to sea, we can travel my way!"

CHAPTER THIRTEEN:
THE WAR IN HEAVEN
BEGINS AND ENDS

THE BOSS SAT watching the battle in Heaven. As he watched, he saw "War" fighting "Peace." He also saw "Life" fighting with "Death." "Hate" was fighting with "Love" and winged angels and demons were falling from the sky. As he watched, he had a huge smile on his face. Of course he was in his warrior armor to impress the other soldiers of Heaven. Yet, he just sat on his throne and smiled. While the Boss was sitting there smiling, a bright yellow light appeared, and out of it walked Angela.

"I just thought maybe you could use some company." Angela said.

"Sure, have a seat." The Boss replied.

"Why are you smiling when there is a war in Heaven?" Angela asked, in a wandering voice.

"Because I know something that nobody else knows." The Boss Replied.

"What is it?" Angela asked.

"It is a divine secret that nobody else will ever know." The boss replied.

"You won't be smiling when your son comes to fight you!" Angela exclaimed.

"Yes, I know he will have to be dealt with." The Boss replied.

Gabriel was fighting with the head general of the Dark One. The head generals name was "Despair." Gabriel did not like "Despair," because he knew that "Despair" was why many human beings gave up on life. As the Boss watched the battle rage on, he thought to himself how much of a mess things were in Heaven right now.

"Man, what a mess!" the Boss exclaimed.

"It sure is a mess." Angela replied.

As the Boss and Angela were talking, a dark shadow fell on the whole of Heaven.

"It looks like my son is here." The Boss said.

A huge cloud of smoke and fire appeared in front of the Boss, and out of it came the Dark One!

"Surrender or be destroyed father!" The Dark One exclaimed.

"How many times do I have to tell you son, if I die, you die." The Boss replied.

"If I am victorious in this war, you will be cast into Hell." The Dark One said.

"You won't win, its' already been determined." The Boss replied.

"Join me father and help me destroy the humans." The Dark One pleaded.

"I will not, the humans still have a lot of good in them." The Boss Replied.

"The war may be determined, but, the fate of the male boy has not." The Dark One said.

"That is true." The Boss replied.

"Then I will find the boy and destroy him and take the spectacles!" The Dark One exclaimed.

"Go then, I will not stop you." The Boss replied.

"Once I have the spectacles, your hopes will come to an end." The Dark One said.

"Call off your attack on Heaven, or I will destroy all of your demons." The Boss said.

"Very well, but I will get the spectacles and change the course of the future." The Dark One said.

The Dark One was looking toward the Heavens. His huge deformed body had smoke rolling off it, and his horns looked blood red. He pulled a large red bell from his dark robe, and began ringing it. The bell called all of his demons back to the depths of Hell. The Dark One hated his father, and he hated all living things. He wanted to turn the Earth into Hell. He wanted chaos for the earth! He wanted to see nothing, but, suffering. He knew if he could get the spectacles, he could change the future into Hell. What the Dark One did not know was David and his friends would not be in Hell when he returned! Gathering his dark forces, the Dark One returned to Hell only to find out that his prisoner had escaped. He learned from some of his demons that "Insanity" had taken a nasty fall, and while he was recovering, the human and four spirits had escaped. The Dark One was so angry that he screamed in torment. His voice brought fear to all the demons in Hell, even the worst of the demons.

"Enough of these games, I need the spectacles!" The Dark One shouted.

"I see you are in need of my services my master." "Hate" said.

"What can you do for me?" The Dark One asked

"I can turn the whole town of Santa Claus against David." "Hate" answered.

"What good is that?" The Dark One asked

"They will seek David out to destroy him, and you will have your spectacles." "Hate" replied.

"Go and do your job, but if you fail me I will cast you into the void." The Dark One replied.

"What is the void?" "Hate" asked.

"The void is non-existence, a world of nothing, with no beginning or end, and its' forever." The Dark One replied.

"You mean I will never be able to spread hate again?" "Hate" asked, in a fearful voice.

"It means that you will no longer exist." The Dark One replied.

"I will not fail you master." The demon "Hate" said

After speaking to the Dark One, "Hate" spread his demon wings and took flight for the world of the human beings. After "Hate" left, The Dark One sat on his throne and dreamed of the day when he would see all of the light that shines on the earth disappear.

By now, David and Isaac, along with Sarah, Whiskers and Rocky, were back in the human world, at the grave yard. Once again, David was saved from Hell! David knew he was only gone a couple of hours in human time.

"We need to put the spectacles on him now Isaac!" Sarah exclaimed.

"No, now is a bad time, we need to find a safer place to put the spectacles on him." Isaac replied.

"Is there any place that is safe?" David asked.

"Let me think of a safer place than the graveyard." Isaac replied.

"You need to think of it in a hurry." Sarah said.

"We can go to the house we were born in." Isaac said.

"That's a great idea!" David exclaimed.

So off they went to the house where Isaac and Sarah were born. They headed out of the grave yard and cut through some cornfields. They walked some, and then sat down and talked awhile. Before long it was getting dark, it was about nine o' clock at night. Isaac told them they had to get to the house because it was getting late, and David would have to be home by tomorrow, or his parents would start to worry. They were very close to the house now, when Sarah took Isaac's hand and said,

"We should tell him now Isaac."

"This is not the time." Isaac replied.

"When is the time Isaac!" Sarah exclaimed.

"When he wakes up after we put the spectacles on him." Isaac replied.

"He doesn't know that he is going to die soon, does he Isaac?" Sarah said, in a sad voice.

"No he doesn't, and he won't know until after he wears the spectacles." Isaac replied.

"The Boss said that he would have his first attack of sickness tonight." Sarah said.

"That is why we are taking him to our old house to put on the spectacles." Isaac replied.

"How long will he be close to death tonight?" Sarah asked.

"Only a few minutes, but, that will be long enough for him to wear the spectacles." Isaac replied.

CHAPTER FOURTEEN:

DAVID BECOMES SICK

AFTER REACHING THE house that Isaac and Sarah were born in, they went straight to the living room and sat down to rest.

"I'm not feeling too good." David said.

"How are you feeling?" Sarah asked.

"I feel weak and dizzy." David replied.

David tried to get up, but, when he got up, he passed out and fell on the floor. Isaac looked at Sarah and told her that he was going to put the spectacles on David. Isaac took the spectacles from his pocket and put them on David. David felt as though he was traveling through a long dark tunnel. He tried to stop, but, could not stop traveling. At the end of the tunnel he saw a light. He passed into the light. He thought that he was dead, and in Heaven. When David took another look, he saw a white horse with wings coming towards him. He was scared at first, but, when the horse landed it began talking to David.

"I am a spirit from Heaven and have been sent here by the Boss." The horse said.

"Am I dead?" David asked.

"No, you are close to death, but not dead." The spirit replied.

"What do you want from me?" David asked.

"Just hop on my back and I will show you." The spirit said.

David got up on the horses back, and the horse took off like the wind. The horse took David back in time. When the horse stopped, it stopped by a tavern that was open in the 1800s.

"Come into the tavern with me, I want you to see something." The spirit said.

"Are we invisible?" David asked.

"Yes." The spirit replied.

They went into the tavern and the horse took David to a table where two men were seated.

"Listen." The spirit said.

So, David listened and heard one man telling the other man that Abe Lincoln had to die! The man talking had hate in his eyes. The other man listening also had hate in his eyes.

"Why are they so angry at Lincoln?" David asked.

"They don't like the changes he has made." The spirit replied.

"Why?" David asked.

"They were happy with the way things were." The spirit replied.

"Where does anger and hate come from?" David asked.

"It starts out as sadness." The Spirit replied.

"What do you mean?" David asked.

"You are wearing the spectacles, listen to his soul not his mouth." The spirit said.

David looked again at the man who was doing the talking. This time he concentrated harder than before. The man's mouth was moving, but his soul was talking!

"Lincoln has ruined my life with his new laws, he has hurt people I love, and that hurts me."

"You see, anger and hate always start out as sadness." The spirit said.

"Why does it become hate?" David asked.

"It's easier to hate, than to deal with the sadness." The spirit said.

"In my History class, my book says that they killed Mr. Lincoln." David said.

"Yes, by killing him they created more sadness and more hate." The spirit replied.

The spirit, in the form of the white horse, told David, that when people are angry, they are really sad, but they can't handle the sadness, and it turns to hate. The horse stopped talking and acted as though it was listening to something. Then it said to David.

"Come on, we have to get you back into your body."

David hopped back up on the horses back, and they took off. The next thing you know David wakes up back in his body. Isaac and Sarah asked David how he was feeling.

"I feel weak." David said.

"Come on, we will get you home." Sarah said.

"When you get home tell your parents you are sick." Isaac said.

"Why?" David asked.

"You are very sick David." Sarah said, with a sad look on her face.

"What's wrong?" David asked.

"You will find out when your parents take you to the hospital."

"I'm scared." David said, looking as if he were going to cry.

"We know, but, we will be with you all the time." Isaac said.

"We will take care of you David." Sarah said.

Isaac knew that David would die at the hospital, and then be revived by the staff.

David began his walk home with Isaac and Sarah helping him walk, and Whiskers and Rocky leading the way. David was very weak by the time he got home. When he came through the door, his mother was getting ready to give him a hug, and David collapse. David's mother began shouting for her husband.

"John, come here right now!"

"What's the matter?" John asked.

"David just passed out!" Judy shouted.

David's father came running towards the front door. When he saw David, he immediately got on the telephone and called for help. The ambulance picked David up, and took him immediately to the hospital. David was admitted to the hospital and put on oxygen. The doctors ordered blood test for David. Isaac and Sarah, along with Whiskers and Rocky, waited in David's hospital room to comfort him. Outside in the hallway, Mr. and Mr.'s Skinner were talking with the doctor.

"We think David may have cancer." The doctor told them.

"My God!" Mr.'s Skinner said, in a fearful voice.

"Is he going to die?" Mr. Skinner asked.

"We think we can stabilize him for now, but we need to know if it's cancer."

Mr.'s Skinner began crying. Mr. Skinner hugged her and told her that David would be fine, but, he had doubts about his son living through the night. David was in the hospital bed having difficult time breathing, and he looked pale and sick.

"Will he die tonight?" Sarah asked.

"No, he will not die tonight." Isaac replied.

"When will he die?" Sarah asked.

"He will live for less than a year." Isaac replied.

While Isaac and Sarah, along with Whiskers and Rocky, continued to spend time in the hospital with David, "Hate" was in the town of Santa Claus Indiana looking for a body to possess. He wanted to pick someone of importance, so when he spread his hate, people would listen to him. In the meantime, while "Hate" was seeking a body, David took a turn for the worse! His breathing became harder, and suddenly his breathing stopped. The heart monitor that he was hooked up to began to beep, and the heart beat signal on the screen went flat! A nurse came into the room and saw that David's heart had stopped! She ran out of the room and down the hall shouting for help! When she reached the desk she called a code blue to David's room. David's spirit was already leaving his body by the time the doctor and other nurses got to the room. David found himself floating upward, out of the room.

Back in the town of Santa Claus, "Hate" found a perfect body. The body belonged to a minister of a local church. "Hate" was in the church watching the minister give his sermon. No one in the church could see "Hate," because he was a spirit. While listening to the sermon, "Hate" became ill.

"How can they believe these lies about the Boss?" He thought to himself.

Only the Dark One can bring them happiness, he told himself. Suddenly, a bright light came through one of the stained glass windows in the church. The light shone directly on "Hate." From out of the light came a form. The form was that of an angel. The angel had fire for eyes, and bright golden armor on. The Angel had a shining silver sword. The angel sat down next to "Hate."

"Hello old friend." The angel said.

"What do you want from me Love?" The demon asked.

"I was just wandering what you were doing in a church." The angel replied.

"I have decided to change my ways." The demon said with a grin on his face.

"What kind of trouble are you going to start now?" The angel asked.

"That is none of your business." The demon replied.

"If you don't tell me, I will make it my business anyway." The angel said.

"Why do you always have to stick your nose in my business?" The demon asked.

"You are my brother "Hate." The angel replied.

"You want to join with me and create peace don't you?" The demon asked.

"Would that be such a bad idea brother?" The angel asked.

"Go away brother, I have business to take care of." The demon said.

"I won't let you possess that minister." The angel said, in a stern voice.

"Why do you think that there will ever be a happy medium between us?" the demon asked.

"Everything in existence has an opposite." The angel replied.

"There is only me brother." The demon said.

"There are more than just you brother." The angel replied.

"Look around in this world; you see wars, murder, and chaos." The demon said.

"Yes, that is what you bring to the human race." The angel said.

"Yes, I turn human against human, nations against nations, and life to death." The demon said.

"Leave the boy alone brother." The angel said.

"The boy is just another piece of meat too me." The demon said.

"David is dying." The angel said.

"When did this come about?" The demon asked.

"He is dying as we speak." The angel said.

"You win brother; nobody will hate a boy that is dying." The demon replied.

"Thank you for listening to me brother." The angel said.

"We have been at odds since the beginning of time; maybe someday we will create peace." The demon said.

"That is what I am praying for my brother." The angel replied.

"I must return to Hell and tell the Dark One the boy is dying." The demon said.

"Goodbye my brother." The angel said.

The angel turned back into a ray of light, and went back up through the stained glass window, and headed for the "Land of the Good." His brother, the demon spread his wings, and flew to the front of the church altar. He then made himself visible to the church members. The church members could not believe what they were seeing. They were so scared they could not move. "Hate" looked at them as he perched by the altar. His wings flapping and the horns on his head had smoke coming from them. He smiled and revealed his long teeth, which were jagged and sharp.

"You all are nothing but animals heading for death, I am your God, I am the truth the way and the light!" The demon cackled.

After he spoke the demon raised his mighty arms and began laughing, as he laughed the foundations of the church shook. The demon stuck his long forked tongue out and then, he vanished. The church members and the minister got into a group and comforted each other. The minister no longer had to convince his congregation that demons existed.

In the meantime, back at the hospital, David was fighting for his life. The town of Santa Claus was going about their business as normal, and had no idea of what was going on in the unseen world around them. As David lay dying, he could hear voices of other children calling for him.

"Come over the wall David, come over and play with us." The voice spoke.

Back at the hospital, the medical staff began working with David to save his life.

David wanted to climb over the wall, but a voice told him it was not his time. So, David did not try to climb over the wall, instead he waited. In the hospital room, The Skinners' were sitting out in the lobby praying that he would make it through the night. Mr.'s Skinner was thinking of the day when she brought David home from the hospital after he was born. She thought to herself how fast the time had passed. She was going over memories in her mind about every year that David was on this earth. Mr. Skinner was holding her hand, and praying.…

CHAPTER FIFTEEN:
DAVID MEETS THE BOSS

DAVID'S SPIRIT FLOATED out of the hospital room and up through the roof of the hospital. Soon, he was up with the stars. After floating among the stars for awhile, he saw a star that was much bigger than the other stars. When he reached the big star, he stopped floating and began falling down towards the star. When he landed on the star, he noticed that he was not hurt from the fall. David looked around after he stood up, and saw a land of crystal blue lakes, mountains, and waterfalls! There was a summer breeze blowing, and he found himself standing in a field of the greenest grass he had ever seen! David began walking towards one of the waterfalls, when he noticed another child walking towards him. The child had black hair and green eyes. The child walking towards David seemed to be about the same size as he was. The child was smiling. When the child reached David, he told David that he had been waiting for him.

"Who are you?" David asked.

"I am the Boss." The child replied.

David looked confused. The child saw the look of confusion on David's face and laughed.

"Why do look so surprised David?" The Boss asked.

"I guess that you don't look old enough to be God." David replied.

"This is just the form I took for you." The Boss said.

"I thought you would have long white hair and a long beard." David said.

"I am anyone and everyone." The Boss replied.

"What do you mean?" David asked.

"Spirits have no human form David." The Boss said.

"Why don't you have a form?" David asked.

"Because I don't need any kind of form, I'm a spirit." The Boss replied.

"Are you a man or a woman?" David asked.

"I am neither." The Boss answered.

"You have to be something!" David exclaimed.

"I am not trapped in the world you live in." The Boss said.

"What is the world I live in?" David asked.

"It's a world that has a category for everything and everyone." The Boss replied.

"What does that mean?" David asked.

"That means I have no gender or race, I'm not bound by those things." The Boss replied.

"I don't understand." David said.

"When you die, you are released from the trappings of life, you are free!" The Boss replied.

"Am I dead?" David asked.

"Yes David, you are dead only for a short while." The child answered.

"Why am I here?" David asked.

"Because you have some things that you need to learn David." The Boss replied.

"Like what?" David asked.

"Take my hand and walk with me, and I will show you." The child said.

"What will I see?" David asked.

"You have the spectacles on, you will see the truth." The Boss replied.

David took the Bosses hand and they began walking towards a circle of light. The circle of light had many different colors in it. David and the Boss walked into the light, and traveled through time. The Boss and David could not be seen by the ghost's of the past, present, or future. The Boss took David from the beginning of time, all the way up to the end of the world. David saw many things while wearing the spectacles. He saw empires rise and fall. David saw wars begin and end. The Boss showed David the sadness of the families though time, who lost loved ones in wars. David saw death, and he saw new life come and go while walking with the Boss through time. David and the Boss traveled though times of plagues that took thousands of lives.' He saw the day he was brought home from the hospital as a newborn, and how happy his parent's were to have him. He also traveled into the future with the Boss, and saw flying cars' and cities with domes covering the entire city. He saw travel to other planets, and many other things. Somewhere in the future, the Boss froze time to talk to David.

"What did the spectacles tell you about the beginning of wars?" The Boss asked.

"They all start with people getting their feelings hurt, and then getting angry." David replied.

"Why do they get angry David?" The Boss asked, in a child like voice.

"They are hurt, so they want to hurt someone else." David replied.

"That is the reason why wars start and people die." The Boss said.

"Will it ever change?" David asked.

"If humans find another way to deal with the hurt, things could change." The Boss replied.

After talking awhile the Boss told David that he had one more thing to show him. Once again a circle of light appeared, and The Boss and David walked into it. David saw the end of the world through the spectacles. Before he could say anything he began to fall downward, as if falling off of a building. It seemed to David like he was falling for a long time, when suddenly, he woke up in his hospital bed. David had a smile on his face when he opened his eyes.' His mother put her arms around him and started crying. His father breathed a sigh of relief. His parents did not know at that time, David only had less than a year to live. David saw Isaac and Sarah, with Whiskers and Rocky standing in the doorway of the room.

"We are leaving now David." Isaac said.

As David looked at Isaac, a tear came to his eye. Isaac told David that they would be back to visit him as soon as they could, but, for now, they had to return to the "Land of the Good." Isaac and his sister, along with Whiskers and Rocky walked out to the hallway and disappeared. David looked at his parents and told them that he wanted to go home. Mr. Skinner told David that as soon as the doctor released David, they would bring him home. David stayed in the hospital for a week. After a week the doctor called the Skinners and had them meet him at the hospital. The Skinners arrived at the hospital around noon the day after the doctor called them. The doctor had bad news for the Skinners. The doctor met them in the lobby of the hospital, and from there, took them to his office.

"Please take a seat." The doctor said.

Mr. and Mrs. Skinner took a seat, and waited to hear what the doctor had to say.

"We have David stabilized enough for you to bring him home." The doctor told them.

Mrs. Skinner sighed with relief over the good news. The doctor told the Skinners that David's health would get worse over the next few months of his life, and eventually, the disease he had would kill him. After hearing what the doctor had to say, Mrs. Skinner broke down and cried. Mr. Skinner knew that he had to stay strong, so he just put his head down, and sat there.

David went home with his parent's, but he missed Isaac, Sarah, and Whiskers and Rocky. He was having good days and bad days. He remembered what the Boss had shown him, and was telling everyone he could talk to, about the experience he had while at deaths door. David was happy to be back in his own bedroom, and was looking forward to attending his school again. For the first few days that David was home, he visited the graveyard a lot to see Isaacs grave and think of past times with his friends. He really missed his friends a lot, and the summer was ending. Soon David would have to get ready to go back to school. He knew that he felt bad, but wanted to get back to school anyway. As usual, things were happening that David was unaware of!

Chapter Sixteen:
Hate Returns to Hell

After leaving the church, the demon, "Hate," went back to Hell to report what he had found out about the boy named David. Once he returned to Hell he went before the Dark One and spoke,

"The boy is not going to live long." "Hate" said.

"You fool, the boy will live for months!" the Dark One said.

"Do you want me to get the spectacles from the boy?" The demon asked.

"The Boss took the spectacles from the boy after he showed the boy everything." The Dark One said, becoming even angrier.

"Then why do you still care about the boy?" "Hate" asked.

"Do you how many people the boy could talk to in a few months?" The Dark One shouted.

"What do you want me to do now?" "Hate" asked.

At this time, the Dark One stood up from his throne in Hell, and let out a hideous scream. The Dark One was flapping his burnt and tattered wings, while at the same time pounding his fist on his chest.

"Do I command an army of fools?" The Dark One shouted at "Hate."

"No master." "Hate" replied.

"Kill the boy and kill his body so his mouth cannot bear witness to what he has seen!" The Dark One shouted.

The Dark Ones shout shook the bowels of Hell so much, that all the demons in Hell stopped torturing souls long enough to cover their ears and hide in fear.

"As you wish master, I will kill the boy's body immediately!" "Hate" replied, shaking in fear.

The demon "Hate" did not waste time leaving; he spread his ugly wings and flew in the direction that would take him out of Hell and into the world of humans. "Hate" flew up through the gates of Hell and headed straight for Santa Claus Indiana. When he arrived in Santa Claus Indiana, he began looking for a body to possess. After looking around for awhile, he spotted a minister. "Hate" knew if he could possess somebody who was trusted and respected, he would have a better chance of killing David. The minister was grocery shopping when "Hate" spotted him. Since "Hate" was a spirit and a demon, he could not be seen by human eyes,' so, he just flew into the grocery store, and perched upside down on one of the ceilings. "Hate" could sense that the preacher was dishonest, and was taking people for their money. He knew the preacher was a fake, which made it easy for him to possess the minister. The minister was reaching for a loaf of bread when "Hate" entered his body. The minister fell to the floor in agony. One of the store clerks thought the minister was having a heart attack, and called an ambulance. The EMS arrived on the scene, and put the minister on a stretcher. The ambulance took off and headed towards the hospital. The minister was a large man, who was somewhat over weight. He had red hair, and green eyes, he also had a red beard and mustache. His name was

Bernie Johnson. The EMS technicians hooked him up to the life support monitor, and he showed no signs of life. Bernie had no heart beat, he wasn't breathing, and he looked very pale. The emergency technicians tried to revive Bernie, but they failed to get his heart beating. One of the technicians named Cindy, called the hospital and told them that Bernie was gone. Once the ambulance reached the hospital, they took Bernie's body down to the morgue. Bernie's body was now alone in the morgue, and "Hate" was laughing about the situation he was in. "Hate" planned this whole situation, so he could bring Bernie's body back to life, walk upstairs to the hospital and appear in front of the EMS technicians, and the nurse on the first floor. "Hate" knew that it would scare the life out of them; suddenly, Bernie's body came back to life and took the elevator up to the first floor. When the elevator door opened, one of the emergency technicians was talking to the nurse at the nurse's station. Bernie walked up to the nurse's station, and tapped the technician on the shoulder.

"Why did you leave me lying on that slab down there in the morgue?" Bernie, who was in reality, "Hate," asked.

"You can't be here, you're dead!" The technician shouted in fear.

"That's funny, I don't feel dead." "Hate" replied.

"Hate," along with Bernie's body, walked down the hall and out the exit door. The technician was scared to death, and the nurse had fainted. When "Hate" was walking through the parking lot of the hospital, he was laughing very hard. He couldn't get over the look on the technicians face. Now "Hates" mind was on finding the boy named David, and ending his life, but first, he would have to find out where he lived. The Dark One was so angry, he told "Hate" to find the boy on his own. "Hate" knew that while he was spending time finding this boy, he would not be able to possess other humans, so the hate level in the world would go down, and his brother "Love" would be working overtime. He knew he would have to work fast so he could get back to his usual job of spreading hate. However, this was a nice rest for "Hate," and he wasn't sure if he wanted to go back to his old job, after all, he had a good job, but it was for eternity, and sometimes it felt more like a prison, than a job. Maybe after he killed the boy, he would disappear for awhile, and let another demon do his job. Yeah! He thought to himself, maybe I could get a little vacation! "Hate" headed for town. He knew that he had to take on the role of a minister, and that some people would know him as Bernie. Being a minister, he could get more information from people, as to where the boy lived. None of the town's people would suspect that a minister would kill an innocent child! He could get away with the murder easily. "Hate" knew Bernie was a Baptist minister, so he went looking for the church that Bernie preached at. After walking for awhile, "Hate" stopped in a gas station in town and asked politely for a phone book. He browsed through the pages of the phone book until he found the phone number and address for the only Baptist church in town. After walking for awhile, "Hate" found the church, and found the addresses of all the parishioners in the church; however, he did not find David's name in the address book. After thinking awhile, he decided that since tomorrow was Sunday, he would preach his sermon, get in good with the church members, and asked some of them if they knew where David lived.

In the meantime, back at the Skinner home, Mr. Skinner knew that David only had a short time to live, so he decided to talk to David and asked him if there was anything he wanted more than anything else in this world. Mr. Skinner wanted David to have his biggest wish come true while he was still living. He thought maybe David would like to go on a special vacation, maybe take a cruise on the ocean, or visit another country. Anything that his son wanted, he would do his best to make it happen. Mr. Skinner talked to his wife, and she agreed with her husband.

Back at the Baptist church, "Hate" was working on his sermon for the service Sunday morning. He was feeling sick writing about God and love. He wanted to write about killing and death. However, he had to appear like he really cared about the people at the service, so he could get what he needed to kill the boy. After he finished writing his sermon, he left the church and went to a fast food restaurant. He arrived at the fast food place, and sat down inside and ordered a fish sandwich and fries, along with a soft drink. While sitting there he saw a young married couple, who looked like they were happily married. "Hate" looked at the couple, his eyes' turned red and he blinked them at the couple. Suddenly, the couple began arguing over things like money, and other things, that really were not that important in life. "Hate" loved to get people hating each other, happiness made him sick to his stomach! Thinking back to all of the wars, needless death, and suffering he had caused throughout history, "Hate" was very happy with his accomplishments. "Hate" was one of the most powerful demons indeed!

"So what if the kid was dying, he would just hasten David's death." "Hate" thought to himself.

"Hate" knew that if he failed the Dark One, he would have to go back to hopping bodies, and causing misery for the human race, or worse yet, be cast into the void!

Chapter Seventeen:
David gives his Last Request

M R. SKINNER AND his wife went up to David's room. David was lying on the bed thinking about his adventures with Isaac and Sarah. When his parent's came into the room, David sat up and looked at them.

"Is something wrong?" David asked.

"Nothing is wrong David; we just want to talk to you." Mr. Skinner replied.

"Talk to me about what?" David asked.

"Your mother and I realize that you have been through a lot." Mr. Skinner said.

"We thought you might have a special wish." Mrs.' Skinner said.

"You mean like something I want to do more than anything else in the world?" David asked.

"We mean exactly that." Mr. Skinner replied.

David told his parent's that he would like everybody in town, including the ministers of all the churches in town, to have a town meeting, because he had something that he wanted to tell them. After hearing David's request, the Skinners looked confused.

"Are you sure that is what you want?" Mrs.' Skinner asked.

"That is what I want." David replied.

"When do you want this meeting to take place?" Mr. Skinner asked.

"I want the meeting to take place in December of this year." David replied.

"Why do you want the meeting in December?" Mr. Skinner asked.

"I will not be alive by the time January gets here." David replied.

"Don't talk like that David!" Mrs.' Skinner exclaimed.

"You both know it is the truth." David said.

Mrs.' Skinner began to cry.

"Don't cry mom, I'm not afraid to die." David said.

"It won't be easy, but you will have your meeting in December." Mr. Skinner said.

As the night time drew near, David got out of bed and put his clothes on. He walked down the stairs and went out to his front porch. His front porch had a lawn chair on it, so he sat down to rest. David was taking radiation treatment for his cancer. He was getting sick to his stomach a lot, and losing some of his hair. The Skinner's front yard had many trees' in it; however, the trees' did not block David's view of the stars. David liked looking at the stars, because they reminded him that earth was just one place, and other places existed besides the one he lived in. After the experiences he had with Isaac, he knew that this life was not the only life, and when he died, he would live again in another existence. There was a nice warm breeze blowing, and it was a starry night. David thought about dying, and he was more worried about his parent's than he was about himself. He was feeling weak a lot, but he tried not to let it get him down. David had a message to pass on, and he would live until he delivered it! Since David spent so much time hanging around with his spirit friends, he didn't spend any time with his human friends, and since he had become ill, the kids in his neighborhood seemed like they looked at him in a different way. His friends didn't come around much since they found out that he had cancer. David also thought about school. He knew that he would not live through another year of school, but he was going to keep going to school as long as he could. Maybe, he thought to himself, his parent's would have another child, and that would help them to cope with his death. David knew that each and every human being was important. He knew this, because he knew that whenever any person got sick or died, it caused sadness on everyone that was attached to that person. David remembered what the Boss had told him. The Boss told him that anger came about when a person refuses to accept sadness. He also told David that anger only made things worse. From what David had seen there had been a lot of anger throughout history! The Boss told David that when anger turned into hate, that is when the wars start, and when other bad things happen. After thinking and looking at the stars for awhile, David smiled, because he knew the most important thing the Boss showed him would be told to a lot of people at the town meeting in December. David's spirit friends were gone now; however, he knew in his heart they were real. He knew that the Dark One would try to kill him before he even got to the town meeting. The Boss would be watching the whole situation, so, David was not afraid.

While David was sitting on the porch thinking, his mother came out and sat down beside him.

"What are you thinking about David?" Mrs.' Skinner asked.

"I'm thinking about a lot of things." David replied.

"What is the most important thing you are thinking?" David's mother asked.

"About how much I will miss you and dad." David replied.

"You will always be with us David, no matter what happens." David's mom said.

"I will never get to go to college." David said, in a sad voice.

"What do you want to be when you grow up?" David's mother asked.

"I wanted to be a pilot." David replied.

"You do not know for sure you are going to die David." His mother said.

"I will never meet a girl, get married, or have kids." David continued.

"You need to stop talking like you are already dead!" David's mother exclaimed.

"I just have this feeling deep in my gut that my life is coming to an end." David said.

"Feelings can be deceiving David." His mother replied.

"Look at me mom, I'm pale, losing my hair, and have red spots all over my body!" David exclaimed.

"You are also taking medical treatments." His mother replied.

"I will try to be more positive mom." David said.

"Come in the house and watch a movie with me and your father." David's mother said.

"Can we have popcorn with the movie?" David asked.

"Your dad is making some popcorn as we speak!" David's mom exclaimed.

David went back into the house with his mom, but, he knew in his heart he would be gone before January of the following year. David and his parents' watched a movie and ate some popcorn. After the movie David kissed his mom and dad goodnight and went to bed. While asleep in his bed David dreamed of being with his spirit friends again, in a place where pain and sorrow didn't exist! Mr. and Mrs.' Skinner tried not to think about the situation for the rest of the night, but found it impossible to keep David's illness out of their minds. The night ended, and the dawn came. The sun was high in the sky, and the sky was a deep blue. A soft wind blew through the screen in David's bedroom window, and reached his face as he was waking up. David thought to himself how lucky people were, who were not sick and dying, and wandered if they woke up each morning counting their blessings. Another day was upon David, and he would fight the illness that was eating away inside of him. He would try to look for the good things in this day, and not worry about tomorrow. No matter how sick he felt he would try not to be a burden on his parents. In another month, school would start, and he would have to worry about his friends feeling awkward around him, but, if they were really friends, they would try to understand what he was going through. David got up and put his jeans and a shirt on, and proceeded to go downstairs to breakfast and begin another day.

Chapter Eighteen:
The Destruction of Hate's Plan

"Hate" was greeting his congregation as they came through the door. What the congregation did not know, was that "Hate" had called on his friend "Doubt," to help him get information on the boy he was sent to kill. "Doubt" was a powerful demon in his own right. He had caused a great deal of suffering throughout history. Whenever people had the right answer to a question, "Doubt" would enter their soul and cause conflict. "Hate" was going to introduce "Doubt" as an assistant minister, and let him preach a sermon. "Doubt" had entered the body of a man the night before. "Doubt" had flown out of Hell when "Hate" called on him for help. He was not picky about the body he possessed, he took the first one he could find, the problem was that the body he possessed was that of the town drunk. "Hate" made "Doubt" shave and put on a suit for the church service. When everybody in the congregation was in the church, "Doubt" began his sermon,

"Welcome people, I'm the assistant minister."

The congregation could not figure out why the town drunk was now an assistant minister, they were so surprised that they paid close attention to the minister as the sermon began.

"Can anyone honestly tell me what God has ever done for them?" "Doubt" asked.

Every one had a confused look on their face.

"Has God ever made your house payment?" "Doubt" continued.

The congregation could not believe what they were hearing!

"Do we really have proof that God exist?" "Doubt" asked.

The town drunk was Roy Wentworth. He was a thin man, and stood about six feet tall. His teeth were yellow, and his eyes' were a blood shot red. Roy, who in reality was "Doubt," told the congregation that they would be better off giving up their belief in a higher power, and start depending more on themselves. He also told them that the Bible was a fairy tale written by people thousands of years ago because they needed something to believe in. As Roy continued talking, a child walked into the church and sat down. The child listened for awhile, and then raised his hand. "Hate" became suspicious, and "Doubt" didn't know quite how to take the interruption.

"What do you have to say?" "Doubt" asked.

"The truth is that you are born with the knowledge of a higher power." The child said.

"How do you know so much about God?" "Doubt" asked.

"I work for the Boss." The boy said.

"Who do you think you are?" "Hate" asked.

"I am the truth." The little boy replied.

As the little boy was speaking, he began to change. First pure white light came out of his eyes.' The little boy grew very tall. He grew to at least twenty feet! Then the rest of his body turned to a radiant white light; which, hovered over the congregation. The assistant minister, who was really

"Doubt," hid his eyes' in fear. The minister, who was really "Hate" pointed towards the light and shouted,

"You have no business here "Truth.""

"I do have business here." "Truth" replied.

"Leave now, or be destroyed!" "Hate" shouted.

"I guess you will have to destroy me." "Truth" answered.

By this time the congregation was getting scared, some of them got up and headed for the door. While heading for the door, the minister shouted at them,

"You are not going anywhere, until you tell me where to find David Skinner!" "Hate" shouted.

"Doubt" wanted nothing to do with fighting "Truth." "Doubt" left Roy's body quickly, and headed back to Hell! "Hate" knew that "Truth" was very close to the Boss, and he also knew that fighting "Truth" would only lead to his demise. "Hate" called on the Dark One for help. The Dark One heard "Hate's" cry for help, and began climbing out of the pit of Hell. The church grew dark, and the floor of the church began to rumble! "Truth" talked to the people in the congregation and told them to leave. "Truth" told them that Lucifer was coming to the church, and he would kill any human he found when he arrived. "Truth" held "Hate" at bay, while the people in the congregation quickly left the church. The people in the congregation would never forget what they saw in the church that day, and if there was anyone in the church, who doubted a higher power, they certainly didn't anymore!

After "Doubt" had left Roy's body, Roy woke up and looked around. First, he looked at "Hate," and then he looked at "Truth." Roy got up off the floor of the church and talking to himself, he said,

"Man, I must have come here to be saved, and ended up with the DT's instead!"

Roy headed for the door and was headed to the first bar he could find!

"King Addictions owns that mans soul." "Hate" said, smiling.

"That man can be saved." "Truth" replied.

"Do you see how weak and pathetic these humans are?" "Hate" asked.

"You have no compassion." "Truth" replied.

"The Dark One is coming to destroy you." "Hate" said, smiling.

"We shall see if the Dark One destroys me." "Truth" replied.

"Why do you protect humans?" "Hate" asked.

"I protect them because they need protection." "Truth" replied.

"Most humans don't even know you!" "Hate" exclaimed.

"There are some humans left that follow the truth." "Truth" replied.

"Hate" was tired of the minister's body, so he left the humans body and took on his own form. "Hate" had the feet of a goat. "Hate's" body was at least ten feet tall, and was covered with burnt skin. He had huge horns on his head, and his face was pure red. "Hate" had dark eyes' that were black as night. There was nothing but death in his eyes'. "Hate" also had sharp pointed teeth, he used his teeth to dig into the souls of humans and cause them to hate.

"Will you let the human live?" "Truth" asked.

"I killed the minister when I entered his body." "Hate" replied.

"Will you bring him back to life?" "Truth" asked.

"No, the only good human is a dead one." "Hate" replied.

"What of his soul?" "Truth" asked.

"The minister was dishonest, his soul is in Hell." "Hate" replied.

"Can he not be forgiven?" "Truth" asked.

"That is the job of the Boss, not me." "Hate" replied.

A foul smell began sifting through the floor of the church, and the cross in the front of the church turned upside down. The floor started breaking up, and Smoke came up from the openings in the floor. Everything in the front of the church, including the altar, and the stained glass began to decay. Suddenly, up through the floor came a huge decaying hand. The hand alone was the size of "Hate's" entire body. After both of the Dark One's hands were out of the floor, a huge set of dark horns followed. The entire church stank of decay and death. Two huge fiery eyes' followed the horns. Then the face; which was a mockery of life arose from the pit that used to be the floor. The Dark One came all the way out of the pit, and he had to bend down in the church to keep from hitting the roof. The Dark One had hoofs for feet, and three clawed fingers on each hand. When "Hate" looked upon the Dark One, he got down on his knees and worshiped him.

"In the beginning, there was light, and seeing light was bad, I created darkness." The Dark One spoke.

"All worship to you my master!" "Hate" exclaimed.

"I sent you to kill a child and he still lives." The Dark One said.

"I was just getting ready to find out where he was, and was stopped." "Hate" replied.

"Silence fool, you couldn't even take care of an easy job for me." The Dark One said.

"I am sorry master, please forgive me!" "Hate" begged.

The Dark One looked at "Truth."

"What is your business here my brother?" The Dark One said.

"What do you mean your brother?" "Hate" asked.

"Truth" is my brother." The Dark One replied.

"I am the son that obeyed his father." "Truth" said.

"You are being misled by our father." The Dark One replied.

"You are the one who is misled." "Truth" replied.

"Humans do not know you." The Dark One said.

"That is not true." "Truth" replied.

"The only truth is darkness." The Dark One said.

"You are wrong my brother." "Truth" replied.

"I have no time to talk; you must be destroyed so we can kill the boy named David." The Dark One said.

"The child will not die until it is his time." "Truth" replied.

The Dark One was preparing to grab a hold of his brother and drag him into the pits of Hell. Suddenly, the roof of the church was blown away by a strong wind, and a voice echoed down to earth from the "Land of the Good".

"Go back to Hell where you belong, my dark son." The voice said.

"Once again, you persecute me father!" The Dark One shouted.

"You chose to be what you are my dark son, you had a choice." The voice replied.

"Why do you choose "Truth" over me?" The Dark One asked.

"Truth" chose to follow me, and you turned against me." The voice replied.

"Humans care nothing about a God!" The Dark One shouted.

"You are not the one to judge that." The Voice replied.

"I must leave, and continue to spread the truth." "Truth" cut in.

"Go spread the word that in the end, truth will be left standing." The thunderous voice replied.

"You were lucky this time "Truth." The Dark One said.

"How did you get out of Hell?" The voice asked.

"The gate was open." The Dark One replied.

"Your friend "Insanity" had a bad fall not too long ago, and I have the keys to Hell now." The voice said.

"The keys belong to "Insanity!" The Dark One shouted.

"The keys were lost when "Insanity" fell off the mountain." The voice said.

"Give me the keys father!" The Dark One shouted.

"Go back to Hell my dark son." The voice said.

"You cannot force me back into Hell father." The Dark One replied.

Suddenly, the voice ceased to speak, and the light from the "Land of the Good" shone in through the roof. The Dark One could not stand the light, he hated it. The Dark One looked up and roared towards the sky.

"Have mercy on me father." The Dark One pleaded.

"Back to Hell my son!" a voice from everywhere shouted.

The Dark One was not strong enough to stand in the light. Slowly, he began crawling back into the pit in the floor. He held his huge clawed hands in front of his face to ward off the light. Soon, he was out of the church, and on his way back to Hell. The Boss sent the angel Gabriel to make sure the Dark One was through the gates, and back in the pits of Hell. The Boss had the keys to Hell, and would make sure that his dark son stayed locked up in the pit. The Boss knew that he could not stop his dark son from influencing humans, or showing up in a spirit form, but, he could make sure that his dark son's physical being never came back to the world of humans.

Bernie's body was found by one of the member's congregation, who was not at the service on the day of the strange happenings. When the EMS checked Bernie out, they wrote it off as a heart attack. The EMS worker, who saw Bernie's body walking around, thought that he was seeing things, and quit the next day.

"The Boss forced "Hate" back to Hell, and "Hate" continued to creep into the hearts of human beings, and continued to destroy as many people as possible.

Chapter Nineteen:
The Meeting in the Town Square

For David, the hours turned into days, and the days turned into months. During David's final days on this earth, he was able to go back to school. His real friends understood that he was sick and did everything they could do to help him during his bad times. His parent's took him on many weekend trips to different places in the United States. David was making every day count. He would always look at the blue skies, the sun, and the landscape around him. David's mother stayed as strong as possible during David's last days. She watched as David's health became worse every day, and she only cried when she was alone, and David was not in sight. Mr. Skinner also stayed strong. He too saw that his son's health was not improving, but he never showed any sadness in front of his son. Mr. Skinner was working every day possible at contacting priests, ministers, and all the heads of the churches in the Santa Claus area. The church leaders talked to their congregations, and many people were planning on going to the town meeting in December, to see what the child had to say.

About two months after David left the hospital, his Grandmother passed away. David knew in his heart that she was in a better place. David and his family attended the funeral. While at the funeral Mr. Skinner noticed that his son seemed at peace with the passing of his Grandmother. Beth was in the "Land of the Good," and was young and happy again!

When November approached, David's health was very poor. He had lost weight, and was looking pale all of the time, but, he kept trying to keep a smile on his face, even with the cancer. Mr. Skinner had gotten the word out about the town meeting to many people, and expected a huge turnout. Many nights, even when the weather became cold, David would sit out on the porch and watch the stars. When David watched the stars, it let him know that the earth wasn't that big, it was just another planet, and there were many planets in the galaxy. David's senses became sharp. He appreciated the air that he breathed, and every day that he was allowed to live, he thanked the Boss. It started snowing in November, and David made sure that he was outside to watch the snow fall. Mr. Skinner made sure that David was all bundled up, and he went outside with David to watch the snow. David and his dad went for walks down the street in his neighborhood, and talked about a lot of things. Mr. Skinner told David that if he could, he would trade places with David, so his son did not have to suffer anymore. What was amazing to David is a year ago his life was just as ordinary as any other person in his school.

December arrived, and the town meeting was planned for December 20, 2011. During the first part of December, David was really weak. He was hoping that he would get his strength back in time for the town meeting. David knew that he only needed a little time to tell everyone at the meeting what the Boss wanted them to know. The meeting was going to take place in a park located in the center of town. Mr. Skinner along with some of the town's people had built a platform. The platform could hold several people. It could also hold two large speakers, and a microphone. When the 19th of December arrived, David was so weak that he had to be carried around the house. The night of the 19th, David's dad went up to David's room to visit. Mr. Skinner asked David why he wanted a town meeting. David told his dad that he would find out at the town meeting what he had to say. That night in December was very cold, and David had a hard time sleeping. He was thinking about the meeting and how he was going to put into words what he had to say. The following morning Mr.'s Skinner made a big breakfast, and they all sat down at the table together and ate. Most of the day, David played on his computer, and watched movies on the television. The meeting had been scheduled for Seven O'clock that night. At six O'clock, Mr. Skinner put on his coat, and then put David's coat on for him. At six-thirty, they all got in the car and drove to the park. When they arrived, Mr. Skinner was surprised to see how many people had shown up! Mr. Skinner and his wife got out of the car and headed for the platform. Mr.'s Skinner had tears in her eyes,' she was happy about the big turnout, but, sad for her son. Mr. Skinner carried David up to the platform, and sat him in a chair next to his mother. There were several friends and neighbors of the Skinner family sitting on the platform. Mr. Skinner took the microphone, put it up to his mouth and spoke,

"My son has something to say to all of you!" He said.

There were at least five hundred people in the crowd, and after Mr. Skinner spoke, they all became very quiet, and attentive. Mr. Skinner took the microphone to his son, and told him to go ahead and say what he needed to say. David was very weak, but, he took the microphone and spoke.

"When I was dying, in between this world and the next, I saw the end of time."

The crowd was very quiet, and continued listening to this child, who was so ill.

"I saw all the good and bad throughout history." David continued.

Now the crowd was very curious as to what the child had seen, they wanted to know what the end of time would bring. David, who was now gasping for air stopped and caught his breath for a moment.

"In the end, the good wins out over the bad, and everyone will be at peace." David said.

Now some people in the crowd wept, because they believed what this boy was telling them.

"All of the sorrow and pain will be gone." David continued.

David began coughing and was coughing up blood. He looked out at the crowd, and standing amongst the crowd, he saw Isaac, Sarah, Whiskers, and Rocky. They were not seen by anybody in the crowd, because they were spirits. Isaac and Sarah walked up to the platform, and then went over to where David was sitting.

"You did a real good job David!" Isaac exclaimed.

"The Boss is very happy." Sarah said.

"Have you come to take me to the "Land of the Good?" David asked.

"Yes David, it is time." Isaac replied.

Isaac held David's hand, and David's spirit left his body. Mr. Skinner shouted to one of his neighbors on the platform.

"Call the EMS!"

David was no longer in his body; he had gone to a better place. The crowd became silent once again. The message David had given them, was one of hope. Some of the crowd was weeping. They admired this sick child, who cared enough about them to give them such hope! David